George Potter

The People's Edition of the Life of the Right Honourable

The Marquess of Salisbury

George Potter

The People's Edition of the Life of the Right Honourable
The Marquess of Salisbury

ISBN/EAN: 9783337188634

Printed in Europe, USA, Canada, Australia, Japan

Cover: Foto ©Raphael Reischuk / pixelio.de

More available books at **www.hansebooks.com**

The People's Edition

OF

THE LIFE

OF THE RIGHT HONOURABLE THE

MARQUESS OF SALISBURY, K.G.

BY

GEORGE POTTER,

(President of the London Working Men's Association.)

Price One Shilling.

London:

GEORGE POTTER, 14, FETTER LANE, E.C.

—

1888.

THE
MARQUIS OF SALISBURY, K.G.,

LEADER OF THE CONSERVATIVE PARTY.

A BIOGRAPHICAL SKETCH.

PUBLISHED BY

THE CONSERVATIVE CENTRAL OFFICE,

ST. STEPHEN'S CHAMBERS, WESTMINSTER, S.W.,

1885.

THE

MARQUIS OF SALISBURY, K.C.,

LEADER OF THE CONSERVATIVE PARTY.

A BIOGRAPHICAL SKETCH.

ROBERT TALBOT GASCOIGNE-CECIL, Marquis of Salisbury, Knight of the Garter, and Prime Minister of England, was born in 1830, and was the second son of the late Marquis of Salisbury. He was educated at Eton and Oxford University, and both at school and college he was distinguished as a scholar. After making a tour round the world Lord Robert Cecil, as he then was, commenced his political career in 1853, at the age of twenty-three, as member for Stamford, a constituency which has also returned Lord Iddesleigh to Parliament, and for thirteen years worked assiduously as a private member. Natural talent, however, combined with that infinite capacity for taking pains, which is sometimes called the characteristic of genius, soon brought Lord Robert Cecil into the front rank of Parliament men. He had also made his mark in the Press, writing largely for such publications as the *Saturday Review* and the *Quarterly Review*, so that he had during his political noviciate undergone a training as varied as it was exhaustive.

In 1866 the Conservatives came into power under Lord Derby, and Lord Robert Cecil, who had become by the death of his elder brother Lord Cranborne, was appointed Secretary of State for India, the same office held now by Lord Randolph Churchill. In this position Lord Cranborne displayed the same quickness and thoroughness of mind and purpose which had characterized his previous career. His official speeches were remarkable for their pith and clearness, while his urbanity of manner and dignity of presence rendered him universally popular and esteemed.

In 1868 the sudden death of his father withdrew Lord Cranborne from the House of Commons, which he left for a seat in the Upper Chamber, regretted by all parties, who had learned to respect his political integrity and admire his personal abilities. But the Tory leader had only changed the sphere of his usefulness. In the House of Lords he continued, as Lord Salisbury, the life of work which he had commenced as Lord Robert Cecil.

In 1874, when the Conservative party once more returned to office with Mr. Disraeli as Prime Minister, Lord Salisbury again undertook the administration of Indian affairs. Four years after he assumed still higher responsibilities. In 1878 Lord Derby resigned his position as Minister of Foreign Affairs. Lord Salisbury succeeded him, and two months after the new Foreign Secretary accompanied Lord Beaconsfield to the Berlin Congress, where the Berlin Treaty was finally settled through the firmness and determination of the British representatives. Lord Beaconsfield and Lord

Salisbury returned home, bringing "Peace with Honour," after having elevated England once more to her proper position in the Councils of Europe.

Shortly afterwards the two Plenipotentiaries, by a unanimous vote, were admitted to the freedom of the City of London, the Chamberlain remarking in his address that Lord Salisbury's grand-father was a merchant trading successfully in the City of London, and that he could claim descent from no less than three Aldermen. In his reply to the Chamberlain, Lord Salisbury made a pithy and sagacious remark, which at the present moment may well be pondered. "In this country," he said, "more than in any other country, the foreign policy of a Government depends upon the public opinion out of doors. It is not that the Government follow servilely an opinion which dictates their policy to them, but that in the eyes of foreign countries no policy is powerful, no recommendations are respected, unless they are known to be sustained by the free and independent opinion of this country." Tried by this test, the foreign policy of Mr. Gladstone was doomed to failure. It has been consistently condemned at home, and has consequently been neither feared nor respected by the Powers abroad.

Lord Salisbury's tenure of office as Foreign Secretary, compared with that of his predecessor, was thoroughly successful. He was heavily handicapped by the legacy of Lord Derby's four years' mismanagement of foreign affairs, and when he left Whitehall in 1880 the relations of England with European Powers were cordial and peaceful. It was reserved for the party of Peace to plunge the country into war, and to embroil her with every nationality on the Continent.

During the past five years of Parliamentary Opposition Lord Salisbury has firmly established himself in the confidence and good-will of the large majority of his countrymen. His treatment last year of the question of Reform was a marvellous exhibition of political prescience. Very early in the day he had instinctively grasped the whole constitutional crisis, and stood almost alone in the gap to save England from piecemeal revolution. He penetrated the sinister devices of the Birmingham Caucus from the first, and gave the country the earliest possible intimation of the gravity of the political situation. The result was a splendid triumph in policy and principle. The Reform question has been settled by both great Parties in the State in Cabinet Council, and the contention of the House of Lords has been verified and vindicated, in spite of the storms of a hostile agitation.

Take another question, which for two years has attracted much public attention, viz.:—The Housing of the Poor. The greatest impetus perhaps which has been given to its solution for the last ten years sprang from the article written by Lord Salisbury in November, 1883, and published in the *National Review*. He there described in pathetic language the results of overcrowding in large towns, and took the best possible way of discovering the solution of the problem, by moving, at the commencement of the autumn session of 1883, for a Royal Commission to enquire into the whole question. That inquiry was conducted under the auspices of the Prince of Wales himself, its results were embodied in a report, and a Bill, giving effect to its recommendations, was brought into Parliament and carried into law, under the auspices of Lord Salisbury as Prime Minister of England, who had two years before so ably ventilated the subject in the public Press.

In everything tending in a practical way the interests of the working classes Lord Salisbury has invariably shown his sympathy and proved his interest. It was a workingman who first pressed upon his notice the urgent necessity for a Commission of Inquiry into the causes of the Depression of Trade, and the demand which was refused by a Liberal Government was ultimately granted by the Conservatives when they came into office. In the same way he acceded courteously to those interested in the Sugar Bounty question, when they asked for an opportunity to lay their grievances before him, and accorded them a patient and sympathetic hearing. He has declared that of all the home questions there is none so overwhelming in its magnitude as the relations between the well-to-do and the poor. He believes that there is growing every day a greater and a more burning desire that all that is miserable in poverty and struggling should be abated. But his treatment will be founded on the attraction and not the antagonism of classes. To preserve the concord, the credit, the confidence, and the co-operation of all classes is the aim of the Conservative Prime Minister. In his own words, he "believes the true test of statesmanlike measures, the true touchstone of whether they will last and produce permanent benefit to society, is whether the problems are touched with a kindly hand, desirous of promoting concord, and whether, above all, that confidence among all classes is maintained which is vital to our material prosperity, which is indispensable to the life and existence of that industry upon which the substance of millions absolutely depends."—*Speech at Manchester*, April 16th, 1884.

Such is Lord Salisbury. The Empire will have little to fear if it is governed by a man of such high lineage, and of such statesman-like qualities. He has shown that he possesses all the qualifications of a great Prime Minister, and as such he will be hailed by the new democracy, whose equitable enfranchisement he has done so much to strengthen and secure. Upon him has descended the heritage of Bolingbroke and Pitt, of Palmerston and Disraeli, and well is the present representative of the ancient family of Cecil fitted, by ancestry and by personal ability, to carry out the principles and policy of the great chiefs of the National party.

Printed by Mackie & Co. Limited, London, Liverpool, and Warrington.

PREFACE.

HAVING met with so much encouragement and appreciation from the readers of The People's Edition of the " Life of the Rt. Hon. W. E. Gladstone," I have determined to issue a series of lives of eminent Political Leaders.

This series, of which our present issue—The " Life of the Right Hon. the Marquess of Salisbury, K.G."—is the second volume, will be uniform with the People's Edition of the " Life of the Right Hon. W. E. Gladstone, M.P." thus placing in the hands of the people an opportunity of possessing an accurate and unbiassed record of the facts connected with the principal events in the lives of the most prominent statesmen of both parties.

To do this in a thoroughly just and impartial manner would be impossible, were the various actions of statesmen of opposite political views to be criticised from any one standpoint ; hence, I have determined, in order that each statesman may receive the fullest meed of justice at my hands, that these " Lives " shall represent the actions of each statesman in the light of the principles which at the time actuated him, and leave it to the reader to judge those principles as his intelligence or political bias may lead him.

This seems to me the only unprejudiced method of dealing with the subject, and I am confident that I shall have not only the approbation but the support of readers of all shades of politics.

GEORGE POTTER.

14, FETTER LANE, E.C.,
January, 1888.

THE LIFE OF

THE RIGHT HONOURABLE THE

MARQUESS OF SALISBURY, K.G.

CHAPTER I.

BIRTH OF LORD SALISBURY—SKETCH OF THE FAMILY OF CECIL—ETON—
OXFORD—1830 to 1849.

THE subject of this life, Robert Arthur Talbot Gascoigne-Cecil, third
Marquess of Salisbury, was born at Hatfield, in the county of Hertfordshire, on the 13th of February, 1830.

The family of Cecil, which dates back to a very short time after the
Norman Conquest, has attained a noble pre-eminence in English history, and, unlike some families with mushroom titles, it can afford to
dispense with the equivocal honour of possessing as a founder either
a knight or a lacquey whom tradition asserts to have accompanied
William I. from Normandy.

Robert Sitsilt assisted Robert Fitz-Hamon in conquering Glamorganshire for William Rufus. His son was Sir James Sitsilt of
Beaufort, in Glamorganshire, who fell at the siege of Wallingford
" having then on him a vesture with his arms and ensigns in needle-
work, as they afterwards appeared on the tomb of his descendant,
Gerard, in the abbey of Dore." These were the same arms which
were assigned to his descendant, Sir John Siltsilt, by Rufus, and as
are at present borne by the Marquesses of Exeter and Salisbury.

There being no Board Schools in those days, and the art of spelling
being considered by gentlemen almost as derogatory as thimble-
rigging is at the present day, each succeeding holder of the name
diversified the orthography at his own sweet will, so that the name
is found variously spelt as Sitsilt, Sisilt, Sicelt, Syssell, Cyssell,
Cecyle, and Cecil.

The family have been connected with Lincolnshire for centuries; Sir William Cecil, afterwards Lord Burghley (whose nod has become historic), represented the county in Parliament in the reign of Queen Mary, and their seat was—

"Burghley House, by Stamford town."

The great grandfather of the present Marquess is the hero of the romance so well told by Tennyson in his "Lord of Burghley." The story, briefly told, is as follows :—

The young heir of the earldom was benighted near Bolas Magna, a village in Shropshire, and obtained shelter in the house of one Thomas Hoggins, and there he met and fell in love with the daughter of his host. After a brief courtship, and sorely against the mother's wish, he, as a Mr. Jones, married Sarah Hoggins. He built a house in the village, and for two years lived there with his wife without in any way satisfying his neighbours' curiosity as to who or what he was. At the end of that time his father died, and, merely explaining to his wife that he had to go to Lincolnshire, and that she must accompany him, set off for his home; and it was only when his wife had admired the house that he told her who he was, and that she was then a countess. On May 4, 1605, the house of Cecil received a token of Royal regard unparalleled in English history—two sons of Lord Burleigh, Thomas and Robert, both being created earls: Thomas the elder—Earl of Exeter; and Robert the younger—Earl of Salisbury. "Sound judgment in the transaction of business was Cecil's greatest quality, and, after a few years' experience of his eminent ability in that respect, there not only gathered round him a knot of cultivated public men, but the people came to look upon him as a man to be safely trusted and confidently followed." Such is the description given by Mr. J. Bruce of the first holder of the title of Earl of Salisbury, and it might with equal justice be applied to the present holder. The Cecil family have always been distinguished by possessing a large amount of caution and carefulness, and a devotion to the interests of both the country and its sovereign; and, as we go on, the reader will find that the present Marquess in no way derogates from the high standard of duty which his ancestors placed before them.

It is curious that it was under a queen, to whom Queen Victoria has often been compared, that two of Lord Salisbury's ancestors, Lord

Burleigh and the first Earl of Salisbury, upheld the honour and dignity of England in a manner that has never been surpassed either before or since; and that, under a queen once more, we now have a Cecil standing up for the defence of the honour and integrity of our noble Empire. The present Marquess was, as I have said, born on the 18th of February, 1830; he was sent to Eton, and at the age of seventeen was entered at Christ Church College, Oxford, and two years later, in 1849, he took the degree of B.A.

Lord Robert Cecil (as he was then called) when at Oxford distinguished himself in the debates of the Oxford Union, advocating, *inter aliá*, the cause of the drama and the necessity of unity amongst the Conservatives—condemning the endowment of Roman Catholicism in Ireland; the dissolution of monasteries by Henry VIII.; the disestablishment of the Church of England.

That aptitude for business and appreciation of detail which have done him such good service in his subsequent political life were so marked that he held the post of treasurer to the Union Society, in which office his third son has since succeeded him.

Into his private life it is neither my wish nor my province to go, beyond merely marking the salient points which have already been made public : suffice it to remark, that those who admire his public life would find even more to admire in his private life, and that those who differ with him on public questions, can find no *point d'appui* in his private character.

Here 1 must find space, though it applies not to the matter in hand, to protest against those writers who, rather than be but little known, choose that their names should be a very stench in the nostrils of honest men, and who, under the immoral guise of a specious morality, and for the sake of their pocket and of damaging a political opponent, drag unnecessarily before the public the private life of public men.

CHAPTER II.

FROM 1848 TO 1853 THE MARQUESS OF SALISBURY TRAVELLED, VISITING
VARIOUS COLONIES, AND STUDYING ATTENTIVELY THE VARIOUS SYSTEMS
OF GOVERNMENT—RETURNED TO PARLIAMENT FOR STAMFORD—VOTING
AT PARLIAMENTARY ELECTIONS.

AFTER his return from abroad, where he had not only done the usual
amount of travelling considered necessary for the final education of
the young man whose parents are well off, but also visited and studied
the British Colonies, it became a question for Lord Robert Cecil to
find a foothold on the first rung of the ladder in the pursuit he had
marked out for himself, viz., politics.

Just at this juncture, Mr. Harries, who was one of the members for
Stamford, and also President of the Board of Control for India,
resigned both his office and his seat ; and the electors, possibly on
account of old-time association (the Cecil family having, as I said
before, been for centuries intimately connected with that borough),
asked him to stand for that constituency.

The life of every public man contains a number of more or
less strange coincidences, and one of these occurs in the fact of Lord
Robert Cecil, who on two occasions filled with great credit the post
of Secretary of State for India, succeeding at his first outset in political
life a man who filled the then equivalent post of President of the
Board of Control for India.

There is another point which presents itself at this period, and
which it is as well to digress upon to a certain extent, and that is that
in his address to the electors, Lord Robert Cecil sounded the key-note
of the whole of his subsequent political career.

It is as well, I believe, to trace back to their source the main-springs
of a man's actions, and to lay them before the reader before recounting
the various and varied forms in which these principles have subsequently taken shape, and I would therefore call the reader's attention
to the election address issued by Lord Robert Cecil in 1853, and more
particularly to the italicized passages quoted below :

"It is my desire to uphold the same great principles as my predecessor, though, of course, not objecting to make cautious changes as

lapse of time, or improvements in science, or the dispensations of Providence may render necessary." *" It will be my duty, and I shall, if I have the honour of being elected, direct my best endeavours to resist any such tampering with our representative system as shall disturb the balance of reciprocal powers on which the stability of our Constitution rests, and to obtain a due adjustment of general and local taxation under the new commercial system, so as to press fairly on all classes alike in a proportion measured by their just claims, and not by their relative strength.*, I am a sincere and warmly-attached member of the Church of England, and therefore I shall be ready at all times to support any measure which will increase her usefulness, and render the number of her bishops and clergy more nearly equal to her requirements." *" I am anxious to give my best assistance in forwarding those numerous measures tending to social and sanitary improvement, and the amelioration of the condition of the labouring classes, which are often passed by amid the din of mere party politics, but on which the future prospects of the country so largely depend."* These two passages could even now form part of any exposition of policy by the noble Marquess; and there are few, if any, statesmen who can look back to their first step in political life with such a quiet satisfaction in knowing that even their bitterest political opponents cannot but acknowledge a continuous and consistent sequence between the different acts of their public life.

It was as a Constitutional progressist of the highest order that Lord Robert Cecil first appealed to the public—a constitutionalist who would mould our noble institutions to the spirit and requirements of the times, but would not consent to their demolition: it is the same Constitutional progressist who now stands before the public as Marquess of Salisbury.

It was as a social reformer that Lord Robert Cecil entered public life: it is as a social reformer—one who has no inconsiderable record to look back upon—that the Marquess of Salisbury to-day can claim a unique position in the esteem of the non-political labouring classes and their leaders.

And all throughout he will be seen to possess a merit rare indeed at present, that of consistency. Not the pig-headed obstinacy of the man who refuses to see because his father was blind, but the unswerving adherence to a principle devoid of personal profit.

The more democratic our institutions are, the more does such a quality in a statesman become not only desirable, but necessary, because professional politicians, who profess what they are paid for, and believe but in themselves, are coming more and more to the surface, and, unless our country can find strong independent statesmen to repose her confidence in, these same gentry may ere long taint our political life as much or even more than they have done political life in America.

On the 22nd of August, 1853, he was returned unopposed as the colleague of Sir Fred. Thesiger, who subsequently became, under the title of Lord Chelmsford, Lord Chancellor. On Tuesday, January 31st, at the opening of the session of 1854 Lord Robert took his seat.

His first speech was made on the 1st of April, 1854, on the subject of the Oxford University Bill; and Mr. G. E. H. Vernon, who followed him, complimented him on the ability and argumentative nature of his first speech. The Chancellor of the Exchequer (Mr. Gladstone) also bore tribute to the future promise of this maiden effort.

In 1855, on the 7th of June, in the debate on the prosecution of the Crimean War, Lord Robert Cecil, following Sir W. Clay, suggested a mode of dealing with the question of the Black Sea, which, if it had been adopted, would have prevented the action of Russia in 1871 at the Treaty of Paris, and would most effectually have prevented any possibility of the merciless war which occurred in 1876 between Turkey and Russia ever breaking out; but this course of action would have precluded the noble Marquess from securing the diplomatic triumph at Berlin in 1878, and the well-won honours which accrued to him in consequence thereof.

His point is thus described in his own words: "It was that the Black Sea should remain closed as it had been, and that the Sultan should have the power to introduce ships of war *ad libitum* whenever he was in danger, he being the only judge as to the fact whether he was in danger or not. Now, by the development of this idea, the Sultan might be able to introduce an English or French fleet, and keep them in the Black Sea, and so by that means provide a more complete assurance for the security of Turkey than any other that could be given."

On the 4th of June, 1857, he moved for a Select Committee to inquire into the subject of the method of voting at Parliamentary elections.

In doing this he laid great stress on the question of expense, not only to the voter, but to the candidate. At that time elections for county members cost candidates £4,000, £5,000, or £6,000, and then twenty-three out of every hundred voters did not attend the poll, and, according to the Liberal organ (*The Edinburgh Review*), in the general election of 1852, fifty-five out of every hundred electors in large constituencies had abstained from voting. "The reason why the franchise had been exercised in so small a number of cases was to be accounted for by the distance which the voters had to go, by the expense which travelling entailed, and by the circumstance that so many persons were so much engaged as not to be able to spare time to attend at the elections. And if," he remarked further, "the Bill for making payment of travelling expenses penal were passed, it would afford a still stronger reason than any which he had advanced for the adoption of some such measure as I have proposed." This measure was the adoption of the system of election by means of voting papers, and he urged it, not only as a means of diminishing expense, time, and trouble to the voter and the candidate, but also as a means of eradicating another blemish on the then system of voting, *i.e.*, the treating of voters. To use his own words:

"The great offence is treating, and the system of voting papers will absolutely put an end to this abuse. Treating usually takes place when voters are brought up to the poll, and, when persons have put off their affairs and have come a distance to vote, they very naturally expect some refreshment, and candidates and their friends have some difficulty in refusing their requests; but, if it were unnecessary for the voter to leave his home, the occasion for the offence would be taken away. Voting papers would also put an end to the inconvenience of collecting together large assemblies of persons in times of great political excitement, and would relieve us from the scandal of those occasional outbreaks of riotous and disorderly conduct which are a disgrace to our political system. Foreigners remarked with astonishment the disgraceful saturnalia that characterize an English election, and the system of voting papers would put a stop to the scenes of personal violence which sometimes occurred."

On Saturday, July 11th, in the same year, Lord Robert Cecil was married by the Bishop of Oxford to Georgina Caroline, the eldest daughter of the late Baron Anderson, and from this date till the

middle of 1858 the name of Lord Robert Cecil does not figure prominently before the public, but in May 4th of that year he took part
in a debate, on a motion of Mr. Gladstone, concerning the Danubian
principalities, backing up his present antagonist.

One of the most curious circumstances in connection with this
debate is the fact that Mr. Gladstone was met with, and that he
condemned, the very tactics which a few years later he himself, when
Premier, adopted, viz., avoiding a debate on the ground that in view
of a Conference it is unwise for Parliament to interfere.

The Liberal Ministry were in 1858 defeated in their Conspiracy
Bill, and a Conservative Administration under Lord Derby came into
power.

Mr. Disraeli, seeing that another Reform Bill was necessary, though
at the same time he perceived that no two sections of either party
were agreed as to the scope of any such Bill, tried to promulgate a
measure which would do effective service and yet not be unacceptable
to the majority of the members. In this it is needless to say he was
unsuccessful.

Two members of the Ministry resigned for diametrically opposed
reasons—one, because the Bill was not wide enough in its provisions
—the other, because it was too wide. Mr. Gladstone even opposed it
because it went too far in a particular direction.

Lord Robert Cecil made a capital speech on this occasion. "He
admitted that the question was surrounded with difficulties of an
extreme character. The working classes naturally felt sore at having
this privilege denied them by an arbitrary line being drawn ; it was
certainly felt by them hard that they should be excluded by a £10
franchise, and those who came nearest to the line thus drawn
naturally felt it a great privation. But it was necessary to draw the
line somewhere, and, however low it was taken, there would always
be a class below it as discontented as the last." He then proceeded to
point out the illogical position of those who opposed the Bill because
it did not go far enough. "He called upon those supporting this amendment to consider the course they were taking, and to ask themselves
whether supporting a mere party move was a course reconcilable to
their patriotism or their consciences. Those who sat above the gangway did not mean the same as those who sat below it. It was clear
that the public opinion on which they relied to discredit the Govern-

ment Bill was not the public opinion with which they sympathized, or which would support them hereafter. Every meeting which had been held had advocated measures which the hon. members opposite would refuse to grant.*All the great towns had called for manhood suffrage, triennial parliaments [cries of ' No, no ']. He repeated the assertion ; Nottingham, Manchester, and all the Metropolitan boroughs had spoken in favour of every principle advocated by Mr. Ernest Jones, and it was quite clear hon. gentlemen opposite would not grant them." This was a home truth, but the idea of reform of any kind coming from the Conservatives was too repugnant to the Liberals, and though they have never since even attempted to grant the demands of the public meetings they had convened, they voted against Disraeli's measure, and the Government were defeated by 330 to 291. The Ministry thereupon dissolved Parliament, and though at the polls they gained a number of seats (29), still they had not enough to enable them to contend against the various sections which by courtesy are denominated the Liberal Party.

A vote of want of confidence in the Government was proposed by Lord Hartington, and carried by a majority of thirteen. A modern historian who aspires to be a recorder of facts, but who has only succeeded in as far as his book exhibits his talents as a novelist, dealing with this subject, remarks : " The result surprised no one. Everybody knew that the moment the *various sections* of the Liberal party *contrived a combination*, the fate of the Ministry was sealed." The italics are my own. Unconscious truths tell most : and no more apt illustration of the *unity* of the Liberal party can be found than in the expression, " Various sections contrived a combination."

The Queen sent for Lord Granville, declining to make an invidious distinction between Lord Palmerston and Lord John Russell; but Lord John Russell refused to hold office under Lord Granville, but elected to heal an old sore by proffering his services to Lord Palmerston if he (Lord Palmerston) were called upon to take office.

In 1860 the Government brought in a Bill for the repeal of the paper duties, which Lord R. Cecil opposed, observing " that what the House had to decide was whether they preferred a paper duty or a 1d. income tax. In his opinion the duty had marks upon it which placed it low in the list of duties which should be remitted. Its repeal would have no sensible effect upon the diffusion of useful knowledge and education, though it might benefit paper makers and publishers. Why was ;it an untenable tax ?   It was increasing, not falling off. The Commissioners of Inland Revenue objected to it because of the difficult cases brought before them. But he looked upon the Report as made to order.   He diverged into details upon the subject of direct and indirect taxation, arguing that, according to every principle of sound finance, all classes ought to pay alike, and, if so, the indirect taxation of the country ought to be increased, not diminished, and therefore the paper duty should not be repealed."

In spite of all opposition, the Bill passed the House of Commons, but was rejected in the House of Lords by a majority of eighty-nine.

This, of course, provoked the usual vituperation of the Lords, though, equally as a matter of course, their decision was ultimately accepted.

In 1861 Lord Robert Cecil busied himself with matters relating to Poor Law administration, the Church of England, and Civil Service, and was one of the prominent debaters with regard to Mr. Gladstone's sleight of hand dealing with the paper duties.

On two occasions has Mr. Gladstone taken up a position which is best expressed by a variation of an old quotation—

" Fiat voluntas mea, ruat cœlum."

The first of these occasions was with regard to these same paper duties, when, his proposition for their repeal being rejected by the Lords, he incorporated the measure with the Budget proposals, thus withdrawing the question from the consideration of the Upper House.

The second occasion was when the House of Commons had rejected his Bill for the Abolition of Purchase in the army, whereupon he effected his object by means of the Royal Prerogative.

In 1862, Lord Robert Cecil made no prominent figure in the outside political world, but gave himself assiduously to the prosecution of his duties as a legislator.

CHAPTER III.

LORD ROBERT CECIL MAKES HIS MARK IN EUROPEAN POLITICS—SCHLESWIG
HOLSTEIN—THE GERMAN NATIONAL PARTY—AUSTRIA'S OPPOSITION TO
REFORM—THE CROWN OF DENMARK—THE TREATY OF LONDON.

THE German Diet having undertaken the cause of the Duchies of
Schleswig and Holstein, Lord Robert Cecil wrote an article in *The
Quarterly Review* for January, 1864, in which he shows that the alleged
wrongs of the Duchies, even taken in their worst light, are but a shallow
pretext for German aggrandizement. He begins by a general sketch
of European events since 1815, pointing out that the Vienna plenipotentiaries, after the ineptitude for self-defence which Prussia and the
smaller German Powers had shown during the great war, were
pardonable in not foreseeing any danger to the balance of power from
the ambition of these same States; but, he adds, "contempt is said by
the Indian proverb to pierce the shell of the tortoise, and the ignominious part which Germany played during the great war had the
effect of awakening a national spirit which had never existed before."

Had this newly-awakened national spirit been well and soberly
directed all would have been for the best, but it exceeded its legitimate
limits, and, "after the fashion of many other nations, during the
course of the last half-century they fed their imaginations upon
historical illusions. They studied the records of the past to find
materials for dreams of the future. They dwelt upon the thought of
what a German emperor once had been; and they sighed for a mighty
German Empire, based upon pure democratic principle, that should
again give law to Europe."

" In order to effect this a naval force is necessary, and this deficiency
the Germans hastened to supply at the earliest opportunity and by
every means in their power, even private subscription being resorted
to; then again, even granting a navy, good harbours in strategical
positions are necessary, and these Nature had denied to Germany;
but the Duchies possessed " a set of admirable harbours both upon the
Baltic and the North Sea," and "if the Duchy of Schleswig and the

Duchy of Holstein could be fairly got into German hands and made subservient to German interests, the whole state of the case would be altered."

" Upon these grounds alone it would not be uncharitable to conclude that the Germans were actuated in the present dispute by very much the same motive as that which actuated Ahab in his celebrated controversy with Naboth. But this imputation, disgraceful as it is, is not matter of surmise; it has been openly admitted or rather loudly proclaimed." " ' Without these Duchies,' say the Committee of the House of Representatives at Berlin in 1860, 'an effectual protection of the coasts of Germany and of the North Sea is impossible, and the whole of Northern Germany remains open to a hostile attack as long as they belong to a power inimical to Germany.'

" A more simply formulated reason for stealing your neighbour's property was never, perhaps, before printed in a State paper."

" The speakers in the recent debate (December 1, 1863) in the Prussian Chamber have not been less plain - spoken. . . . . von Twesten : ' The Duchies are for Germany and Prussia a strong bulwark under all circumstances against any attack coming from the North. This as well as their maritime position are advantages Prussia can never relinquish. . . .' Dr. Löwe : ' What interest has Prussia in the London Protocol ? Since the time of the Great Elector, Prussian policy has always been rightly directed towards gaining the North German Peninsula for Germany.' The extract is curious: both as an admirable specimen of the morality current among the German patriots of the present day (1864), and also for the calm audacity with which the new geographical designation of North German Peninsula has been invented."

" But it hardly needed these frank confessions to enlighten us upon the subject. No one who has followed the Schleswig-Holstein controversy carefully and impartially can entertain even a momentary doubt that he is reading over again, in a more tedious form, the fable of the Wolf and the Lamb."

The article then proceeds to describe the specific grounds on which the Germans built their specious claims. In 1830, the German desire to annex the Duchies first became apparent, and a new doctrine was elaborated which is known by the name of the Schleswig-Holstein theory.

According to this theory, Schleswig and Holstein had been united for four hundred years under the King-Duke, and were independent of the rule of Denmark proper. Thus Holstein being part of Germany, and Schleswig being indissolubly united to Holstein, it followed that Schleswig-Holstein was part of the great fatherland. It never seems to have occurred to them that the argument was capable of being turned round. If Schleswig is Danish, it follows, according to the doctrine of indissoluble union, that Holstein must be Danish too. But there never was a definitive union; this is sufficiently demonstrated by the fact that it was very seldom that either of them could keep its own unity—let alone any right to be united with its neighbour.

It would be endless to describe the various combinations into which they were cut and carved at various periods of their history: sometimes they were under two princes, sometimes under three; at one time under as many as nine; sometimes they were united with the Danish crown, and sometimes they were separated from it. Sometimes one of them was united and the other was not; or bits of each were united to it, while bits of each were severed from it. Until the last alienated morsel relapsed to the Danish monarchy in 1779, there were only two periods in the course of their long history during which they were united under one prince; one of these periods lasted for fifty-five years, the other lasted for twenty-one, and the most recent of them was more than three centuries ago. Since then they have never been combined independently of the kingdom of Denmark proper. Before 1779 they were not (with those two exceptions) ever combined at all. Since 1779, until this controversy began, they were under the absolute government of the King of Denmark and had no independent rights at all. Anything less like "a union of four hundred years, independent of Denmark proper," cannot well be conceived.

The "Charters" invoked by the German party in support of their case are then shown to be of an equally unreliable character. "This part of the German case is so curiously weak, that it is often difficult to believe that any man, having a reputation for common sense to lose, should have seriously advanced it. There are two points to be proved: first, that the two Duchies are by right independent of Denmark; secondly, that they are indissolubly united together.

In support of the first the "Constitution" of King Waldemar is invoked. King Waldemar was a boy of twelve, who usurped, or rather was put upon, the throne of Denmark for four years, and the only evidence of the existence of such a Constitution is a parchment, without date of place or seal, which purports to be a letter written in 1448 (one hundred and odd years after the date of King Waldemar) by a Count of Oldenburgh, who was subsequently elected King of Denmark. In this letter, written apparently for the purpose of securing his election, the Count says he has been shown a number of documents, one of which contains a Latin passage signed by King Waldemar III. and his Council, and dating from A.D. 1326. The Latin passage runs thus:—" *Item Ducatus Sunderjutiæ regno et coronæ non unietur nec annectetur ita quod unus sit dominus utriusque* " (" Also that the duchy of South Jutland (Schleswig) shall not be united with nor annexed to the crown and kingdom in such a manner that there shall be one lord to both ").

This Constitution, granting its genuineness, only provides that Denmark and Schleswig shall never be ruled by the same king. "In other words, it promises that an arrangement which, in regard to parts of Schleswig, has existed for four hundred years, and in regard to the whole of it, for a century and a half, which has been sanctioned by the Congress of Vienna, and has never been called in question by the Schleswigers or the Germans themselves, shall never take effect."

Now with regard to the "indissolubly united" question, the "charter" appealed to is the "Privileges" of King Christian I. The passage bearing on the subject is as follows: "That the lands shall remain for ever together undivided." But the Privileges also provide for separate legislative bodies, for separate judicial tribunals, and for separate administration ; so according to the Privileges the only way in which they could be intended to be "for ever together undivided" was by dynastic unity. This was the groundwork of the agitation until 1848, when the King of Denmark granted to both Denmark proper and the Duchies a free Constitution. This would have bound the Duchies still more to Denmark, and therefore it did not suit the National Party of Germany. A revolution was organized, and the revolutionists were supported by Prussian troops ; but in 1850 Russia brought pressure to bear, and Prussia withdrew, the only condition being that Denmark would leave the pacification of Holstein to the German Diet. Accordingly, in February, 1857, an Austrian and

Prussian army occupied Holstein for the ostensible purpose of pacification, but with the firm intention of not withdrawing until some sort of ransom had been paid.

Now Austria hated the National Party, but she had a still greater dread of a German community, as free as England, living on the north bank of the Eyder. "Terrified at the prospect of an active liberal propaganda, composed of exiles from every German state, conspiring, printing, haranguing, actually within earshot of Germany, she resolved to nip that danger in the bud; and it was intimated to Denmark that a guarantee against the incorporation of Schleswig must be a condition precedent to the restoration of Holstein."

From this date the question resolves itself into a study of despatches, protocols, and treaties.

The despatches resolve themselves into the one point that Austria demanded, that the King of Denmark should not extend to the Duchies the free Constitution he had granted to Denmark proper. The protocols contain the per contra undertaking that the Powers should be solicited to confirm the succession of the then reigning family of Denmark, and the treaties embody both.

In 1861 another agitation arose in Holstein, and the King of Denmark offered to the Holsteiners a charter granting them an amount of civil liberty exceeded in no country in the world—full freedom of the press, unlimited right of association, a Habeas Corpus Act of extreme stringency, responsibility of officials to the ordinary tribunals—these were the baits offered to the Holsteiners to induce them to come back in to the Danish Constitution, under a representative system of the ordinary type. But this would not suit the National Party, and Count Berstorff admitted, in 1863, that the Holstein sore was being kept open purely for the purpose of forcing Denmark to yield upon the subject of Schleswig.

But now another complication comes upon the scene. The crown of Denmark had not until 1670 become hereditary, but during the reign of Frederic III. the Lex Regia was passed, by which female heirs of that monarch could inherit as soon as the male succession was exhausted; and under the Lex Regia the wife of Prince Christian of Glückstein became queen, and she renounced her rights in favour of her husband. The question now arises—Did the Lex Regia apply to the Duchies?

If not, on the hereditary principle the Duke of Augustenburg would be the king, as he is the eldest male descendant of Christian III. (1559), but, unfortunately, the hereditary principle was not established till 1670, so that the Duke of Augustenburg is 111 years late for reaping any benefit in that way; and further, the late Duke, in consideration of £400,000, renounced all claim to either estates or power in these words—"We moreover promise, for ourselves and our family, by our princely word and honour, not to undertake anything whereby the tranquillity of his Majesty's dominions and lands may be disturbed, nor in any way to counteract the resolutions which his Majesty might have taken, or in future might take, in reference to the arrangement of the succession of all the lands now united under his Majesty's sceptre, or to the eventual organization of his monarchy." This was in 1853, and it was not until 1859 that the present Duke of Augustenburg thought fit, after the money had been paid, to protest against it.

The Treaty of London was after that renunciation drawn up and signed. The Treaty is in the names of the Emperor of Austria, the Prince President of the French Republic, the Queen of England, the King of Prussia, the Emperor of Russia, the King of Sweden, and the King of Denmark; other States were subsequently invited to accede, and Saxony and Hanover, amongst others, consented.

The case foreseen came to pass—the male line of Frederick III. died out—and in conformity with the treaty France, England, Russia, and Sweden at once recognized Prince Christian as his successor ; but Austria and Prussia hung back—Saxony and Hanover, overjoyed at being allowed to play a conspicuous part of any kind, be it ever so ignominious, loudly proclaim that they are not only willing, but eager, to dishonour the faith that they have pledged.

These small States show a method in their madness, as they are tolerably safe from punishment. Their wisdom in trying to precipitate a conflict in which, individually, they can hardly lose and may possibly gain, may perhaps be justified by the event. Saxony, for instance, will probably in any case reverse the fate of Francis the First, and escape with everything except her honour. The article then proceeds to argue that England is bound by honour to see that her treaty promises are upheld, and to hold her co-signatories to their word. "Let Germany see distinctly that war with Denmark means war with

England, and the Governments that are now weakly yielding will draw courage to free their subjects from the imminence of a greater danger. But promptitude and courage are above all things necessary. In every portion of Europe the combustible materials lie scattered ready for the match. If they are kindled into war, no human power can set bounds to the conflagration or predict the limits of its rage. Upon the action of England, who alone desires peace, the continuance of peace depends."

CHAPTER IV.

IMPORTANT CORRESPONDENCE UPON GERMANY AND DENMARK BY LORD
ROBERT CECIL, COUNT VITZTHUM, AND LORD ROBERT MONTAGU.

THE article quoted in the preceding chapter seems to have flurried
Count Vitzthum von Eckstaedt, the Saxon Minister at the Court
of St. James, as on January 3rd he sought an interview with Mr.
Disraeli. "I begged him," says Count Vitzthum in his "Reminis-
cences," "to tell me candidly whether Lord Robert Cecil's warlike
article in *The Quarterly Review*, as well as the anti-German language
of the Tory papers, generally corresponded with the view intended
to be maintained by the Conservative Party in Parliament. Disraeli
replied emphatically in the negative, and assured me that Lord Robert
Cecil had only expressed his private opinion." This had the effect
of reassuring Count Vitzthum.

Professor Forchhammer, however, who had been defending the
German view of the matter, was unmercifully "sat upon" by the
following letter :—

LORD R. CECIL UPON GERMANY AND DENMARK.

To the Editor of THE TIMES.

(Published Jan. 22, 1864.)

SIR,—I regret that in consequence of absence from town I have not
been able sooner to reply to the letter which Dr. Forchhammer,
Professor of the University of Kiel, has addressed to you in reference
to some remarks of mine that appeared in your columns. Much,
however, of his letter does not require further discussion, inasmuch as
it has been fully answered by your correspondent "H. T. P." Much,
also, of the Professor's letter is beside the question at issue. The
grievances under which he alleges that the Schleswigers suffer, the
restraints upon their press and upon their right of meeting, may or
may not be well founded.

This may be the fault of the Danish Government or of the German
Opposition ; but in any case they are not matters of international
complaint. Denmark has not promised to Germany that she will
give the Schleswigers a free press ; and, except in those cases in which

Denmark has bound herself by positive promises to govern Schleswig in a particular manner, no foreign Government has the shadow of a right to interfere in the internal politics of that Duchy.

The Germans have, or believe themselves to have, a right to protest against all laws which favour the Danish Schleswiger to the disadvantage of the German Schleswiger. But that right exists, if at all, only by virtue of certain stipulations which were alleged to have been made in 1852. This limited right does not give the German Powers any sort of title to interfere in respect to other laws which they may or may not approve, but which apply to Dane and German equally.

If, indeed, the German Powers are entering upon a general crusade for the freedom of the press and the freedom of association, they may not pay much regard to the limitations of their legal right; but in that case it would be better to begin with their own race in Livonia or Alsace, and they may even find a profitable field for their efforts within the limits of the Confederation itself.

At a moment when war is impending, the only questions of interest are those out of which, in appearance at least, it is likely to arise. The Diet goes to war to defeat the Treaty of London, Austria and Prussia go to war to defeat the Constitution of November last; and these two points are, therefore, the only ones that are of importance now. Professor Forchhammer's mode of dealing with the Treaty of London is very popular in Germany, but it is absolutely unintelligible in England.

He simply inveighs against that treaty, and appears to imagine that when he has done so he has made it less binding on those who signed it. The treaty is attacked because it was concluded without the assent of the Diet, of the Assemblies of the Duchies, and of a certain number of the Agnates. There was a good reason for omission in each case. The Diet was not consulted, because Austria and Prussia, who did sign the treaty, were at the time its mandatories in respect to the affairs of Holstein, and the idea of a Diet which should set Austria and Prussia at defiance had not occurred to the statesmen of that day. The Assemblies of the Duchies were not consulted, because they were provincial bodies, of modern origin, and of a competence strictly limited by their charters, which gave them no authority to deal with questions of succession. The mass of the Agnates were not consulted, because the Duke of Augustenburg, who

stood first in that line of succession, had renounced his claim for a
large sum of money; and his renunciation was held, according to
certain well-known European precedents, to be abundantly sufficient
to bar those who claimed through him. It is not sufficiently remembered upon the German side that but for this rule the Emperor of
Russia would be the rightful heir of Kiel. Either an heir, by
renouncing his claim, can bind those who claim through him, or he
cannot. If he can, then the renunciation made by the Duke of
Augustenburg in 1852 bars his son Prince Frederick. If he cannot,
then the renunciation of his undoubted right to Kiel made by the
Emperor Paul, in 1773, does not injure the title of the present
Emperor Alexander.

Either way, Prince Frederick has no right to the homage of
Professor Forchhammer at Kiel. Every Englishman must concur
in the strong language which your correspondent "H. T. P." has
used with respect to the conduct the pretender and his father have
jointly pursued in the matter of this renunciation. " We promise for
us and our family, by our princely word and honour, not in any way
to counteract the resolutions which his Majesty may have taken, or in
future might take, in reference to the arrangement of the succession
to all the lands now united under his Majesty's sceptre."

So wrote the Duke of Augustenburg in 1852, and received full payment for the promise. In 1863 he executes an act of renunciation in
favour of his son, especially for the purpose of enabling that son
to upset the succession which eleven years before he had pledged himself "not to counteract." He receives money in consideration of a
special promise; he breaks the promise, but he does not refund the
money. If "the Germans of moral character," to whom Professor
Forchhammer appeals, approve this mode of dealing with a " princely
word of honour," I can only express my surprise.

Even, however, if these objections were as strong as they are weak,
they would be worthless now. The fact that the consent of the Diets,
the Estates, and the mass of the Agnates had not been obtained, was
as patent in 1852 as it is now. Austria, Prussia, Würtemberg, and
Hanover knew of it as well as they do now; and yet they signed or
adhered to a treaty in which those consents were not so much as
mentioned. If they may not plead an alleged omission, which they
carefully forebore to notice then, as a ground for dishonouring their

signatures, no security can be attached for [the future to any international obligations.

There is no treaty in existence about which it may not be pretended that some adhesion was not obtained which ought to have been obtained. The last point noticed by Dr. Forchhammer is, perhaps, the most important, as it is the one upon which Austria and Prussia have elected to go to war. The assertion that the Constitution of November last " tends to incorporate " Schleswig with Denmark is constantly made, but the exact point in which this tendency appears is never specified. No attempt has been made to define this momentous word " incorporate," upon which the issue of peace and war are made to turn.

There are several degrees of combination in which two different communities constitutionally governed may exist together under the same sovereign ; and these degrees are marked by the relative position of the legislative bodies in each. There is the purely dynastic union, where each community has its own legislature, co-ordinate and independent. There is the Federal system, where common affairs are managed by a common assembly, and provincial affairs by a provincial assembly, each being, within the limits of its own competence, independent and self-subsisting. There is the anomalous system of our own empire, in which one supreme Parliament controls a cluster of subordinate parliaments. And, lastly, there is the complete combination to which the metaphor "incorporation " is more properly applied, and which takes place when the local or subordinate assembly is altogether superseded, and the central Parliament assumes the entire government. The Irish Union is a case in point. The second of these— the Federal system—is that which is sanctioned by the Constitution of November. The provincial Parliament of Schleswig is independent, and within its own sphere supreme. The tie that binds Denmark to Schleswig could only be made looser than it is by converting it into a purely dynastic union ; and no one can read the correspondence of 1851–1852 without seeing that a dynastic union was the last arrangement contemplated under these engagements. A common assembly for common affairs, and local assemblies for local affairs, is the brief description of the scheme sketched out in that correspondence ; and it is also a true description of the Constitution of November. Austria and Prussia have not pointed out what the objections are which they take to that measure, nor have they stated in what other way they require that the relations between Denmark and Schleswig shall be adjusted.

They are going to war, in short, for a vague metaphor which they refuse to define, and in order to establish a state of things in Schleswig the nature of which as yet they are not able to describe. And they attach so much importance to these objects, that they decline to forego them even for a few weeks till a European Conference can decide upon them! Under such circumstances it is not to be wondered at that their sincerity is regarded with suspicion.

I have the honour to be, your obedient servant,

ROBT. G. CECIL.

This was too damaging to the German cause to be left to an uninterested party to answer; so Count Vitzthum, " being sure of the discretion of the chief editor of *The Times*," set to work to reply under a *nom de guerre*.

COUNT VITZTHUM TO THE EDITOR OF *THE TIMES*.

(Published January 23, 1864.)

GERMANY AND DENMARK.

SIR,—Lord R. Cecil's letter, which you printed in *The Times* to-day, contains assertions so utterly inconsistent with the facts, that, in the interests of truth, you will allow me to point out some of the most glaring errors, which, if not contradicted, might prevent your readers arriving at a fair and unprejudiced view of the case. I trust the noble lord himself, who, unwittingly and in perfect good faith, I am sure, has committed these errors, will admit the fairness and, upon inquiry, the truth of the following corrections :—

I. Austria and Prussia did not act as mandatories of the German Diet, when they signed, on May 8, 1852, the Treaty of London. Both signed that treaty on their own account as European Powers. No Austrian, no Prussian statesman has ever thought of denying this fact.

II. The Diet was not consulted, because the signatories had every reason to doubt whether they would be able to carry the consent of that body to an arrangement which is considered as utterly inconsistent, not only with German, but with international law, because the assents of the interested parties have not been obtained.

III. The claim of Russia with reference to certain parts of Holstein (the so-called " Gottorpsche Antheil," including Kiel) is not recognized in Germany as founded in law, because, in consequence of the nego- tiations (of 1750–73), the Imperial House of Holstein-Gottorp, which now reigns over Russia, have exchanged their claims on the " Gottorp- sche Antheil" against the counties of Oldenburg and Delmenhorst. Should they desire to rescind that arrangement, and revive their title with regard to certain parts of Holstein, they would be obliged to restore the equivalent which they received for it—viz., the dominions of the Grand Duke of Oldenburg. This they cannot do, because the Grand Duke, according to the Treaty of Vienna, has become a Sove- reign Prince, perfectly independent of his cousin, the Emperor Alexander.

This will be sufficient to show that the pretensions of Russia, assumed in the Protocol of Warsaw, will be found, after further in- vestigations, utterly abrogated by the Treaties of Vienna.

IV. The Duke of Augustenburg by his declaration, or, as it is wrongly called, his "renunciation," could never bind his eldest son, for the simple reason that this son was of age already in 1852. To make the Duke's "renunciation" lawfully binding on Prince Frederick, the assent of the latter was wanted. The Danish Government, by an oversight which would appear strange, were this the only fault of omission they committed, have never thought of asking Prince Frederick's adhesion, and he has never put his name to any paper which could be possibly interpreted as an adhesion or an assent to his father's "renunciation."

If a British peer were to dispose of his entailed property, or even of his rights and expectations to an entailed property which some day may be obtained by him, without the consent of his son, this son being of age, would such an arrangement be perfect and binding on the son, according to English law? I do not know ; but what I do know is that, according to German law, it would be utterly null and void, as far as the son's title and birthright are concerned, provided he had been of age "at the time" when his father thought fit to dispose of his inheritance or his expectations.

V. The Duke of Augustenburg has never "received full payment for the promise " not to counteract the arrangements made for the Danish succession. The money which he received has never been considered, not even by Frederick VII. and his advisers, as an equivalent for any promise, but as an indemnity for the estates which were the private property of the Duke, and which the Danish Government compelled him to sell in a given time, for the same reasons of political expediency which induced the present French Government some years ago to compel the Orleans Princes to sell their private estates in France. The Danish Crown bought land and no promise.

If King Christian IX. would consent to restore these estates to the rightful owner, the House of Augustenburg would be too happy to recoup his Majesty by paying back the comparatively very scanty indemnity which the Duke received in 1852.

I know very well the common report, which says that the Duke was a " rebel," and that as such the King of Denmark had " confiscated " his property. *Væ victis !*

But I think there are in these happy islands many who, if they knew the true history of this " rebellion," would exclaim with Cato, " *Victrix causa Diis placuit, sed victa Catoni.*" The fact is, that there has never been a judgment against the Duke, and that the whole accusation rests upon *ex parte* statements of the Danish Government, who had the power, but certainly not the right, of confiscating the private property of a princely house connected with the reigning sovereign.

I inclose my card, though my name would give no more weight to the foregoing statement, which is based on facts undisputed, as will be easily ascertained.

I am, Sir, your obedient servant,

AUDIATUR ET ALTERA PARS.

Not content with this, he asked Lord Robert Montagu to come to his assistance.

COUNT VITZTHUM TO LORD ROBERT MONTAGU.

HOBART PLACE, *January* 23, 1864.

DEAR LORD R. MONTAGU,—Allow me to call your attention to a letter which appeared this morning in *The Times* under the signature " Audiatur et Altera Pars." This letter refutes the most glaring errors of Lord R. Cecil's composition which was printed in yesterday's *Times*. Still, there is an assertion of Lord R. Cecil which has been left unanswered, viz., "The Assemblies of the Duchies were not consulted, because they were provincial bodies, of modern origin, and of a competence strictly limited by their charters, which gave them no authority to deal with questions of succession."

Every word of this paragraph is an error. The Assemblies of the Duchies were not consulted, because the Danish democrats, who ruled over the King and the State of Denmark, knew perfectly well that the Estates of Schleswig and Holstein would never be fools enough to commit the suicidal insanity of accepting the London Treaty.

These Assemblies were not more "provincial bodies" than the Rigsraad of Copenhagen, where Denmark proper is exclusively represented.

To state that the Estates of Schleswig and Holstein are of "modern origin," and had no competence nor authority "to deal with questions of succession," shows only that the writer has not taken the trouble of studying the question. He would have found that a Parliament which actually exercised its competence and authority, not only to deal with, but to decide *proprio motu* the question of succession in 1460 (in the time of Richard of York), can scarcely be looked upon as one of "modern origin."

If the Estates of Schleswig and Holstein (the knights, prelates, and cities, as they are called) had not had the "competence" and the "authority" which Lord R. Cecil contests, why, the title of the reigning House of Oldenburg would be forfeited, because the Holsteiners and Schleswigers elected Christian I. (of Oldenburg), King of Denmark, to be their Duke, and he—the forefather of all the Holstein branches now living—confirmed the rights and privileges of those "provincial bodies of modern origin" by a letter patent, which goes under the name "Die tapfere Verbesserung," and recognized therein expressly their right to elect another male member of the reigning house, should the heir object to taking the oath which he, King Christian, as Duke of Schleswig-Holstein, took to uphold and to protect the ancient privileges of the Estates.

We have not forgotten in Germany the chivalrous speech you made in June, 1861, in favour of the rights of the Duchies, when you denounced the London Treaty as the London conspiracy, and when a "count-out" was found to be the only means of silencing the champion of right against might. I trust that this year you will find a full House to listen to your manly speeches in favour of a good cause.

Should you want facts, dates, documents, I have an arsenal at your service. For the moment, I think a little skirmishing with Lord R. Cecil would do no harm, and I am certain *The Times* would be most happy to print a statement of yours based on the facts which I have taken the liberty to recall to your mind.

Yours very truly,

VITZTHUM.

The flattery contained in the last two paragraphs was evidently not thrown away, as the two following letters show :

LORD ROBERT MONTAGU TO COUNT VITZTHUM.

January 24, 1864.

MY DEAR COUNT VITZTHUM,—I wrote yesterday, in a very hurried manner, an answer to Lord Robert Cecil's letter, which I had just seen.

In my haste, the passage to which you allude escaped my notice, although the error attracted my attention when I first read his letter. I have therefore sent a short P.S. to *The Times* office.

I fear they will not print my letter, as I am no favourite with the editor, As far as I can make out from the Blue-books, the Duchies (and Germany) do not desire to break the treaty, if only the ancient rights of the Duchies be preserved and their autonomy maintained.

I am sorry that I missed the honour of seeing you when you called. Any information that you may consent to give me, I shall be most thankful to receive.

Yours very faithfully,

ROBERT MONTAGU.

GERMANY AND DENMARK.

(Published January 25, 1864.)

To the Editor of THE TIMES.

SIR,—I had barely two hours, after reading the letter of " Audiatur " in your impression of yesterday, and that of Lord Robert Cecil in the preceding number, to write a few remarks on the inaccuracies which they contained. In my haste, a most serious error in Lord Robert Cecil's letter escaped my attention. He says, " The Assemblies

of the Duchies were not consulted, because they were provincial
bodies, of modern origin, and of a competence strictly limited by
their charters, which gave them no authority to deal with questions
of succession."

Of modern origin! They are as of ancient an origin as our House
of Commons. In 1640 they, of their free and absolute authority,
determined the succession to their throne. What "charters" can
Lord R. Cecil be thinking of? When they elected Christian I. they
required no charter to authorize them; their "competence" was not
then strictly limited to paltry provincial matters. From Christian I.,
the kings of Denmark, the Augustenburgs, and the Glücksburgs have
descended! From him the kings of Sweden derived their origin, and
the Emperor of Russia has come down. Yet Christian I. had to
wait, cap in hand, for the free election of those maligned and con-
temned Diets.

Had it not been for the Assemblies of the Duchies, where would
have been the kingdom of Denmark and the rival claimants to the
throne? When Christian I. had obtained the desired boon, he swore
to maintain the ancient rights of those Duchies; and every king
since his day has taken the same oath, and sworn to maintain their
authority. Now they are set aside as of "modern origin, and strictly
limited competence."

It you will be good enough to append this as a P.S. to my letter of
yesterday evening, or if you will grant it a place in a succeeding
number, you will oblige.

Your obedient servant,

ROBERT MONTAGU.

Lord Robert Montagu was not in time with his postscript to
receive attention at the hands of Lord Robert Cecil, as in the same
paper the following letter disposed of the attempt made by "Andiatur
et altera Pars" to refute him, and at the same time had a nasty sting
in its tail:

LORD R. CECIL UPON GERMANY AND DENMARK.

(Published January 25, 1864.)

To the Editor of THE TIMES.

SIR,—Your correspondent who signs himself "Audiatur et altera
Pars" accuses me of "glaring errors," and of "assertions utterly

inconsistent with the facts." So grave a charge must be my excuse for again troubling you with a demand upon your space, which I have already taxed so heavily. The statements which have been impugned are based upon well-known documents.

It will not be necessary that I should quote them at length. A brief reference to them will suffice to satisfy your readers that my assertions are quite consistent with the facts, and that the error is not on my side.

I. His first correction rests upon a misapprehension of my meaning. I did not say that Austria and Prussia signed the Treaty of London on behalf of the German Diet. What I did say was, that when Austria and Prussia signed the treaty they were mandatories of the Diet in regard to the affairs of Holstein, and that that fact, joined to the then undisputed supremacy of those two States in the Diet, presented to the non-German Powers a sufficient reason for considering that it was superfluous to consult the Diet formally. I do not quite understand whether your correspondent doubts that Austria and Prussia were mandatories of the Diet in regard to the affairs of Holstein at the time the treaty was signed. If so, I can only refer him to the Federal resolution of two months later (July 29, 1852), by which that mandate was formally terminated.

II. The reason which induced the Great Powers not to associate the Confederation with themselves in the Treaty of London may be a matter of conjecture; but the reason which prevented Denmark from asking for its accession at the time that she asked for that of the other smaller Powers is on record. It was simply that England declined to assent to her doing so. In the circular of the Danish Minister, M. Bluhme, of September 9, 1852, the following passage occurs :—

" The Confederation is not to be found among the States enumerated in the enclosed list, because there is reason to believe that, in reference to the invitation of that political body, the contracting Powers will be less unanimously agreed. According to information recently received from the king's Minister in London, it appears certain that the British Government, which looks upon a simple notification as sufficient, will refuse to apply for the accession of the Germanic Confederation."

Simple notification, it must be observed, was the course taken towards the least important Powers. The British Minister of the day probably acted from mere consideration of international etiquette; but, whatever his motives, it certainly could not at that time have been, as your correspondent has imagined, any fear that the Diet would reject a proposal upon which Austria and Prussia were agreed.

III. Your correspondent writes to expose my "glaring errors," and among them he enumerates my statement that Russia, under certain contingencies, has a claim to Kiel—a claim which he says "is not recognized in Germany." I must decline to admit that every fact which is not recognized in Germany is a "glaring error." It is a point of at least equal importance that the claim is very strenuously upheld in Russia, as the readers of recent telegrams may have observed. That either of the disputants for the right to so good a harbour as Kiel should "recognize" the title of the other is an amount of impartiality which few will be unreasonable enough to expect. The dispute upon this matter is a complicated one, like all that belongs to this case.

The material point of it is that the Emperor Paul (then Crown Prince) in 1773 ceded his portion of Holstein, not to the kings of Denmark generally, but only to Christian VII. and his brother Frederick, and their male descendants. Their lineage is now extinct. It seems to be an inevitable result that the cession, which was made only to those descendants, has ceased to be operative. If so, the right to Kiel and some other parts of Holstein reverts to the Emperor Alexander, the heir of Paul. By the Protocol of Warsaw that right is renounced in favour of the present king and his male heirs.

But the protocol expressly provides that if the arrangement by which King Christian was to inherit the whole Danish monarchy should fail, the renunciation of Russia would cease to be obligatory.

IV. The next "glaring error" of which your correspondent accuses me is the opinion that the Duke of Augustenburg, in renouncing his own rights, could bind those who claimed through him. I can only plead that I sinned in good company, for the same view was taken by the Powers who negotiated the arrangements of 1852, and especially by Prussia, who procured the renunciation from the Duke. Nay, I think I can appeal to a higher authority still.

The same view must have been taken by the Duke himself when he wrote the words, " We promise for us and our family not to counteract the resolutions which his Majesty may take in reference to the arrangement of the succession." Your correspondent appears to me to have placed the Duke in a painful dilemma. Either the Duke did believe that he could bind his family when he wrote those words, in which case he was guilty of a "glaring error," or he did not believe it, in which case he was guilty of a gross fraud.

But, at any rate, whether he could bind his son or not, he could certainly bind himself. He did bind himself not to aid any one in disturbing the succession. Had he adhered loyally to his promise he would have refused to make any renunciation in favour of his son, and then Prince Frederick would not have had a shadow of a claim during his father's lifetime.

In reference to the legal argument of your correspondent, I need hardly observe that his appeal to the English law of entail is very far wide of the question. The case must be argued upon European precedents, and not upon English statute law. I need not enter into a question which has been so abundantly discussed. The most important case bearing upon the question, whether a renouncing claimant can bar those who claim through him, is the renunciation of Philip V. at the Peace of Utrecht, and the tendency of that case is directly adverse to the modern German view.

V. The next "assertion utterly inconsistent with facts" of which I have been guilty, is that the money paid to the Duke was paid in consideration of his renunciation. Your correspondent must have forgotten the terms of the instrument (December 30, 1852) in which the renunciation is contained. The first two sections refer mainly to the cession of landed property; the third section contains the promise not to counteract the new arrangements for the succession, which has been so often quoted. The fourth section then runs as follows:—

"The before-cited cession and transfer of our own rights as to the before-cited ducal possessions, &c., as well as the obligations, promises, and assurances before mentioned, undertaken by us towards his Majesty, have been accepted by his Majesty the King for himself and his royal successors to the crown; and he has on his side promised to us, for himself and his royal successors to the crown, the following terms."

Then follows a list of the money payments to be made to the Duke. It requires no argument to prove that only the cessions of land, but also the promises and obligations mentioned in the first part of the section, together constitute the consideration for the money promised in the second.

I need not go further for the purpose of showing what grounds your correspondent has for charging me with "glaring errors" and "assertions utterly inconsistent with facts." I should not have troubled you with an answer to him at this length, but that I am inclined to surmise from internal evidence that he is peculiarly entitled to take a zealous interest in the cause of the House of Augustenberg. I have only to apologize to you for the space I have unwillingly occupied in this reply, and am,

Your obedient servant,

ROBERT G. CECIL.

The sting was evidently felt, as "Audiatur" followed on the 29th idem by the following—denying any intention of a personal attack, and also disclaiming any *personal* interest in the matter :

COUNT VITZTHUM TO THE EDITOR OF *THE TIMES.*

(Published Jan. 29, 1864.)

GERMANY AND DENMARK.

SIR,—In pointing out to you the other day some of the errors which every one who knows something about the question of the day will have detected in Lord R. Cecil's letter of the 21st inst., my object was certainly not to make any personal attack on his lordship, or to wound his feelings in any way. My object was to serve, in my humble way, a good cause—the cause of peace which *The Times* defends so ably and powerfully, let us still hope so successfully—in its columns. With regard to the points at issue, a short commentary on Lord R. Cecil's reply will be sufficient to show that there is still something to say on the other side of the question.

I. The serious German complications which sprang out of the Danish dispute turns on the fact which I stated, that Austria and Prussia did not act as mandatories of the German Confederation when they signed the London Treaty. The consequence was that the new order of succession which that treaty endeavoured to create for the Duchies of Schleswig, Holstein, and Lauenburg has until this day never been acknowledged, not even (until a few days ago, when Sir A. Malet forwarded a copy of the treaty by a note to the Federal President)

officially known by the German Diet. Whether Austria and Prussia
had full powers from the Diet for other definite negotiations respecting
Holstein ; whether those full powers expired in July or in May, 1852 ;
and whether other Powers fancied that Austria and Prussia acted as
mandatories of the Confederation, all this is perfectly irrelevant,
and has no bearing whatever on the important fact that those two
German Powers signed with other Powers a treaty contempla-
ting, for a certain contingency of the future, a new order of succession to be established in a German country without the knowledge,
without the authority, and without the full powers, of the German
Confederation.

II. It pleases Lord R. Cecil to sneer at the Diet, to pooh-pooh the
notion that where the vital interests of a German country are concerned, the central organs of a nation of 40,000,000 to 45,000,000
ought to have been consulted in order to make such an arrangement
lawfully binding on Germany. I may tell the noble lord that he will
scarcely find any statesman in England, with some practical knowledge of what is going on just now in Europe, who does not deeply
regret, if not deplore, that the German Diet has not been consulted ;
that, legally and technically, the Treaty of London does not exist for
Germany ; and that the Danish succession, so far as the Duchies are
concerned, is still an open question, and cannot but be considered by
every German statesman as an open question as long as the Diet
assented. I may tell him, also, that there is in Germany, as far as I
know, no statesman worthy of that name who does not deplore that the
imbroglio brought about by this embryo of a treaty has not been
avoided by the Danish Government, which by a wiser policy would
have found means of conciliating in time the German subjects of the
late king.

The British Government—let me say this for the honour of a statesman who held the seals of the Foreign Office for a few days only—has
not been blind to the danger, which Lord R. Cecil appears still unable
to detect, of not consulting the German Diet, and of not binding
Germany to that treaty.

There will be found somewhere in the [pigeon-holes of the Foreign
Office the draft of a despatch which was addressed simultaneously to
Vienna and to Berlin, urging Austria and Prussia to lay the London
Treaty before the German Diet. And why did Austria and Prussia

not act upon that wise and friendly advice? Was it not to their own interest to do so, in order to legalize the somewhat irregular course they had taken? Undoubtedly it was. But they could not do it, they could not even think of proposing the legal enactment of that arrangement, because they knew perfectly well that as long as all the Agnates and the Estates of Schleswig and Holstein had not given their assent, it would have been out of the question to expect the assent of the German Diet.

III. With regard to the Russian claim, the future will show who is better informed, Lord R. Cecil or myself. All I can say is that newspaper telegrams are not evidence enough for those who happen to know something about the question to induce them to fear that Russia, in the face of certain documents discovered lately, at Kiel I think, and of certain others which are carefully preserved in the State archives of a northern German State, will seriously bring forward claims which, if they were ever submitted to a British lawyer, would be dismissed as utterly worthless.

IV. I have no pretension to judge the Duke of Augustenburg, and I trust the noble lord will fairly admit that there may be still some family documents which might not have been communicated to Lord R. Cecil, and which, if known by him, might perhaps compel him to pass a milder judgment on a foreign prince, belonging to a house connected with almost all the reigning families of Europe. At all events, the Duke of Augustenberg is beside the question. His acts, intentions, motives, have nothing whatever to do with the rights of his son. Prince Frederick was of age when his father signed his declaration without his son's consent. Every German lawyer would have told the Danish Government that any declaration of the Duke could not be binding on the son, being of age. If they have neglected to demand his assent, as they have done, they have only to blame their own carelessness.

V. With regard to the last point, I accept Lord R. Cecil's admission of the 23rd, that "cessions of land" were, after all, made by the Duke of Augustenburg, as refuting the assertions of the letter of the 21st, which said that the Duke "renounced his claim for a large sum of money," and "that he received full payment for a promise," without mentioning the fact that, besides a "claim" and a "promise," some estates were thrown into the bargain, estates which, if sold to-day, would fetch certainly more than the Duke received according to the arrangement of December, 1852.

I may be allowed to add that the noble lord is wrong in surmising " that I am particularly entitled to take a zealous interest in the House of Augustenburg." I have not the honour of knowing either the Duke or the Prince ; I have nothing to lose by that cause, and it is to me personally a matter of perfect indifference whether the German Diet finally recognize Frederick VIII. or Christian IX. as Duke of Schleswig and Holstein, this being still, as far as I know, an open question.

I remain, Sir, your obedient servant,

AUDIATUR ET ALTERA PARS.

I may be thought to have given too much space and attention to the above correspondence, but though the subject may be of little importance to the general world, the correspondence had a marked effect on the future political career of the Marquess of Salisbury, and in fact was the beginning of the second era in his life.

CHAPTER V.

THE COMMENCEMENT OF THE SECOND ERA IN LORD SALISBURY'S LIFE—
NATIONAL SCHOOLS—GERMANY AND DENMARK—NATIONAL EDUCATION—
UNIVERSITY TESTS BILL—GENERAL ELECTION, 1868—PARLIAMENTARY
REFORM—THE IRISH CHURCH—FROM THE COMMONS TO THE LORDS—
GENERAL ELECTION OF 1874—CONSERVATIVE MINISTRY.

THE article in *The Quarterly Review* and the subsequent correspondence in *The Times* did a great deal towards placing Lord Robert Cecil in a higher rank among politicians than he had hitherto occupied. In most other countries a man may become a famous politician by excellence in some particular department, but in Great Britain few obtain more than a mere passing recognition at the hands of the public who do not show a comprehensive grasp of the subjects necessary for the due administrative efficiency of all departments of State. In this controversy Lord Robert Cecil first showed conclusively that he possessed a practical knowledge of other than purely British questions, and, as a natural sequence, he began to forge his way into the front ranks of his party.

This progress in public estimation continued steadily, and in 1865 received an additional fillip by his becoming, on the death of his elder brother, Viscount Cranborne and heir to the Marquessate of Salisbury; and by 1878 he had attained to the highest point but one, *i.e.,* the leadership of his party.

From 1878 he held the position he had acquired till the spring of 1881, when an event occurred which marked the second epoch of his political career, and which I will leave for consideration to a future chapter.

During the year 1863 the Liberal Government gave the country an illustration of their usual policy, so aptly described by Disraeli as "plundering and blundering." The "plundering" was exemplified in the proposal to tax charitable corporations—a proposal which was stoutly combatted by Lord Robert Cecil; and the "blundering" took the form of a dispute with Brazil, in a debate on which subject Lord Robert Cecil remarked that the Foreign Secretary (Earl Granville) seemed to adopt a " tariff of insolence in his correspondence with Foreign Powers."

On March 8th Mr. Adderley moved a resolution reprobating the manner in which the Government dealt with National Schools; and speaking in support of this resolution, Lord Robert Cecil said that " the right hon. gentleman (Mr. Lowe) lost no opportunity of striking at the basis of a system which he had been placed in his present office to administer. What the House had reason to complain of was that the right hon. gentleman did not come forward, when he moved the Estimates, and acquaint the House with the changes, and tell them the effect of his proposals. Instead of doing so, he wrapped his schemes up in those hieroglyphics which the Permanent Secretary of the Treasury knew so well; and in these they remained till some hierophant of the Education Office unravelled them. Then the House found it was not some alteration in detail they had passed, but that some principle which they had cherished, and which was at the foundation of the whole system, had been secretly sapped and undermined." The motion was finally agreed to. But this was not Lord Robert Cecil's only stand for the education of the children of working people, for on April 12th he brought forward a resolution with regard to the mutilation of Inspectors' Reports by the Committee of Council on Education. In his speech he remarked:—

"Now, what the right hon. gentleman the Vice-President of the Committee of Council on Education claims to do, and what I traverse his right to do is this — he claims to expunge from those Reports all opinions which differ from his own. It will be at once plain to hon. members that such a practice entirely destroys the value of the Reports as any guide to the House in the course it should take in educational matters. Nor is this all. What I want to point out to the House is that this is not only an injurious plan, but it is a breach of the original understanding upon which these inspectors were appointed."

Mr. Lowe made a very bitter reply, but the motion was carried by 101 to 93.

On the 12th of April Mr. Lowe resigned in consequence of Lord R. Cecil's motion, and made a personal explanation in the House of Commons. After which Lord Robert Cecil rose and disclaimed any idea of a personal charge against Mr. Lowe, as did also Mr. W. E. Forster, Mr. Walter, and Mr. Disraeli, the latter of whom bore testimony to Lord Robert Cecil's straightforward conduct in the matter.

In July, Mr. Disraeli proposed a vote of censure on the Government for their conduct with regard to the quarrel between Germany and Denmark. On the second night of the debate, Lord Robert Cecil supported Mr. Disraeli's motion, and, after pointing out the pot-valour of the Government, added : "I remember a story of a naval officer who once endeavoured to justify the use of the profane habit of swearing by saying that the men would never think him in earnest if he did not swear : and it seems as though hon. gentlemen opposite thought that unless the Foreign Secretary did not proceed to diplomatic execrations, no expressions of his, however strong, amounted to threats. This loss of dignity and honour is not a sentiment: it is a loss of actual power. It is a loss of power which will have to be bought back at some future day by the blood and treasure of England. . . . If we do not mean to fight, we ought not to interfere. If we do not intend to carry out by arms our threats and measures, we must abstain from the luxury of indulging in them. That is the only policy of the future which is involved in the censure of the Government for the past."

And dealing with the penalties usually incurred by the boastful:— " Look at the difficulty of your situation now. You cannot by any form of words you can use persuade Foreign Powers you are in earnest. In any future European complications that may arise, you may tell them that you are not indifferent to a question, that you view the matter in a very serious light, that the aggressors might be met by armed intervention ; but until you have committed yourselves to irrevocable war, you will not be able to make those listen to whom you address yourselves."

On February 28, 1865, the subject of National Education was brought forward by Sir John Pakington, who moved for a Select Committee to inquire into the constitution of the Committee of Council and the system under which the business of the office was conducted ; and in the debate Lord Robert Cecil disputed the arguments of Mr. Lowe, and claimed for the House of Commons a larger jurisdiction over the Education Department, and a greater control over acts affecting such wide interests as the education and the expenditure of a large amount of public money.   Speaking of the pleasure Mr. Lowe's speech had given him in one respect, he added : " As he (Mr. Lowe) proceeded, his native truthfulness overcame his official discretion."

The motion was subsequently adopted, and a Committee of Inquiry was appointed.

A very slight attempt was made during the Session to deal with Parliamentary Reform, but nothing resulted.

On June 14th Lord Robert Cecil moved to defer the second reading of the University Tests Bill for six months.   The vice of the Bill he observed, was that it would give over the government of the University to Dissenters.   Mr. Goschen had candidly told the House that it would be better to copy the universities of Germany ; that our universities and colleges had no special connection with the Church ; that they were national institutions not connected with any particular form of religion.   But the admission of professors of every form of religious belief to the governing body of the university would introduce an element that would practically amount to the teaching of no religion at all.   This amendment was, however, negatived in a division by 206 to 190, and the Bill was read a second time.   But the Session was far advanced, and the further progress of the Bill being manifestly impossible it was shortly afterwards withdrawn.

On the day that he made the above speech his elder brother died, and the honorary title of Lord Cranborne consequently devolved upon Lord Robert Cecil.

On July 7th Parliament was dissolved, and the Ministerialists gained some seats.

Before the next House could meet, Lord Palmerston died, and Earl Russell succeeded him as Premier.

In 1866 Parliament met on the 1st of February, and one of the first subjects with which the Government attempted to deal was Parliamentary Reform, and on the 12th of March the Chancellor of the Exchequer (Mr. Gladstone) brought in a Reform Bill.   This was stoutly opposed by a member of Mr. Gladstone's own party and by the Conservatives, as it was evident it was framed for the purpose of increasing the voting power in, and the number of members of, those places where Liberal opinions were predominant.

After the Bill had been read the first time, the second reading was fixed for the 12th of April, after the Easter recess.

This interval was, it is needless to say, by the leader of the House of Commons utilized for the purpose of stumping the country *more suo*, and accusing his opponents of being unfriendly to and distrustful of the "working classes."

To the second reading of the Bill an amendment was proposed by Earl Grosvenor and Lord Stanley, and on this amendment Viscount Cranborne spoke. He repelled the charges made against the opponents of the Bill, and said that if Mr. Gladstone had any cause for imputing improper motives to them he should have done so only on the floor of the House. Instead of that, however, he went to Liverpool, and there, before a select company admitted by ticket, he said that the working classes were looked upon by the opponents of the Bill as an invading army. That was not consistent with the obligations which the leader of the House of Commons ought to accept. The odious charge made was that the opponents of the Ministers wished to exclude the working classes from all share in political government. He could quite understand that when he (Mr. Gladstone) had nothing to say for his Bill and nothing to say against the amendment, it was very convenient to shower dirt on those who oppose the measure. His own feeling with respect to the working men was that we heard a great deal too much of them, as if they were different from other Englishmen. He could not understand why the nature of the poor or working men in this country should be different from that of any other Englishmen. They spring from the same race. They live under the same climate. They are brought up under the same laws. They aspire to the same historical model which we admire ourselves ; and therefore he could not understand why their nature should be thought better or worse than that of other classes.

The second reading was only passed by a majority of five, and the Government had to add a Redistribution Bill in order to have even a remote chance of passing their measure. But even with this sop they failed, and on an amendment by Lord Dunkellin they were defeated by eleven, and in consequence resigned.

Upon Lord Derby now devolved the duty of forming a Cabinet, and he offered to Viscount Cranborne the Secretaryship for India. This offer Viscount Cranborne accepted, and on the 12th of July was re-elected for Stamford without opposition, and on the 19th of the same month he made his official appearance in the House of Commons on the occasion of the introduction of the Indian Budget. As Viscount Cranborne had been but a short time in office, the masterly way in which he dealt with the details was the subject of congratulation from both sides of the House, and from none more warmly than from his predecessor, Mr. Stansfeld.

In 1867 Parliament met on the 5th of February, and on the 11th Mr. Disraeli essayed once more to deal with the question of Reform. He wished to adopt the principle of proceeding by resolution first, but in deference to the expressed wish of the House he withdrew the resolution and brought in a Bill.

To the provisions of this Bill Lord Carnarvon, General Peel, and Viscount Cranborne objected, and, in consequence, on the 25th of February resigned.

Viscount Cranborne, in giving his explanation in the House on the 4th of March, stated that he did not think the time was ripe for household suffrage, and therefore he must oppose the Bill.

After many debates and amendments, the Bill received the Royal Assent on the 15th of August.

Beyond opposing this measure, Viscount Cranborne took little part in the politics of this year, being naturally unwilling to damage his party, and, on the other hand, having seceded from the Government, not being in the best of positions for assisting them.

In 1868 Parliament met on the 13th of February, and on the 26th Lord Derby resigned on account of ill-health, and Mr. Disraeli became Prime Minister.

Mr. Maguire, one of the members for Cork, having initiated a discussion on affairs in Ireland, Mr. Gladstone rose and said that it was his opinion that the Church of Ireland as a State Church must cease to exist. Following this declaration up on the 23rd, he (Mr. Gladstone) brought forward three motions dealing with the question of the disestablishment of the Irish Church. Monday, the 30th, was fixed for the debate, which Mr. Gladstone opened with a characteristic speech. He was followed by Lord Stanley, who moved an amendment that such an important question should be left to the decision of a new Parliament. At an early period in the debate Lord Cranborne spoke against the resolutions, and at the same time condemned the Government for not adopting the more manly course of meeting the resolutions with a direct negative instead of trying to shelve the question. Mr. Disraeli, speaking subsequently, said that it would have been impossible to move the previous question, as that implied that the Government did not admit any modification with regard to the Irish Church necessary—which was not the case—and the amendment was framed according to a dictum of Sir Robert Peel, "Never attempt in your amendment to express your policy." On a division the amendment was negatived by 60, and the resolutions were carried by 56.

In consequence of this adverse majority the House was adjourned until the 20th of April.

It was fated, however, that Viscount Cranborne should not again address the House of Commons, for, his father having died on the 12th of April, 1868, on the 7th of May he took his seat in the Upper House as the Marquess of Salisbury.

At this period there is a lull in the political life of Lord Salisbury, not on account of failing activity, but because his field of labour was more circumscribed : yet, though the public did not see the whole of it, an immense amount of unostentatious, useful work was done by him.

When Mr. Gladstone's Suspensory Bill was before the House of Lords, the Marquess of Salisbury opposed it, and deprecated the idea that the Upper House should give way at every display of discontent ; when, however, in the new House of Commons, Mr. Gladstone's Irish Church Bill passed with a majority of 114, Lord Salisbury rose to the occasion and voted for the second reading. His statement as to the relative positions occupied by the House of Lords and the House of Commons is well worth quoting.

" I wish to say a word or two with respect to the position of this House as it relates to the other branch of the Legislature and the nation at large. It has been represented that admitting it to be the duty of this House to sustain the deliberate, the sustained, the well ascertained opinion of the nation, we thereby express our subordination to the House of Commons, and make ourselves merely an echo of the decisions of that House. In my belief, no decision could be more absolutely inconsequential. If we do merely echo the House of Commons, the sooner we disappear the better. The object of the existence of a second House of Parliament is to supply the omissions and correct the defects which occur in the proceedings of the first. But it is perfectly true that there may be occasions in our history in which the decision of the House of Commons and the decision of the nation must be taken as practically the same. In ninety-nine cases out of a hundred the House of Commons is theoretically the representative of the nation, but is only so in theory. The Constitutional theory has no corresponding basis in fact; because in ninety-nine cases out of a hundred the nation as a whole takes no interest in our politics, but amuses itself and pursues its usual avocations, allowing the political storm to rage, without taking any interest in it. In all these cases I make no distinction—absolutely none—between the prerogative of the House of Commons and of the House of Lords. Again, there is a class of cases, small in number, and varying in kind, in which the nation must be called into council and decide the policy of the Government. It may be that the House of Commons in determining the opinion of the nation is wrong, and, if there are grounds for entertaining that belief, it is always open to this House, and indeed it is the duty of this House, to insist that the nation shall be consulted, and that one House without the support of the nation shall not be allowed to domineer over the other. In each case it is a matter of feeling and of judgment. We must decide by all we see around us and by events that are passing. We must decide —each for himself upon our consciences, and to the best of our judgment, in the exercise of that tremendous responsibility which at such a time each member of this House bears—whether the House of Commons does or does not represent the full, the deliberate, the sustained convictions of the body of the nation. But when once we have come to the conclusion from all the circumstances of the case that the House of Commons is at one with the nation, it appears to me that—save in some very exceptional cases, save in the highest cases of morality—in those cases in which a man would not set his hand to a certain proposition though a revolution should follow from his refusal—it appears to me that the vocation of this House has passed away, that it must devolve the responsibility upon the nation, and may fairly accept the conclusion at which the nation has arrived. My Lords, I cannot think that in thus stepping aside we are abdicating our duty, or are showing that want of courage with which we were charged the other night. It is no courage, it is no dignity, to withstand the real opinion of the nation. All that you are doing thereby is to delay an inevitable issue —for all history teaches us that no nation was ever thus induced to revoke its decision—and to invite besides a period of disturbance, discontent, and possibly of worse than discontent. Now, I am jealous of any language which may seem to trench on the prerogative of this House, and I have tried to guard my words against any interpretation which should seem to imply that, in the ordinary course of legislation, there is any inferiority between one House of Parliament and the other. But one of the rare occasions to which I have referred has now occurred. The opinion of Scotland, and Ireland, and I may add, of Wales, is passionately in favour of this measure of Disestablishment. England, though more doubtfully and languidly, is also in favour of the same measure. And looking at these facts and at the general current of opinion ; looking at all quarters of the political horizon and seeing succour in none ; seeing that the opinion of literary men is against you ; seeing that the mass of religious opinion among Dissenters and Catholics is against you ; seeing that what the Foreign Secretary laid so much stress on last year—the opinion of foreigners —is against you, though I take this opinion as not worth much as a guide to our conduct, but as worth a good deal as indicating the tide of opinion—seeing that nowhere is there any appearance of any movement that can reverse the decision of the nation, save in assemblages of which the power has been tried and found wanting—on all these grounds, my Lords, I can conscientiously come to no other conclusion than that the nation has pronounced against Protestant ascendency in Ireland, and that this House would not be doing its duty if it opposed itself further against the will of the nation."

In 1869 (Nov. 12th) the Marquess of Salisbury was unanimously elected Chancellor of the University at Oxford, in succession to the Earl of Derby, who had then just recently died. This office Lord Salisbury has worthily filled, for while a jealous guardian of the privileges of the University, he has always taken a keen interest in forwarding any well-timed and matured scheme of reform.

In 1870, legislation for Ireland first began to monopolize the attention of Parliament, and beyond a Peace Preservation Bill and the Irish Land Act the Session yielded but little fruit. In both these measures Lord Salisbury showed much interest, and his action was conducive to the alteration for the better of many clauses in each.

When Sir John Lubbock's Bank Holiday Bill reached the House of Lords (1871) the Marquess of Salisbury took charge of it, and safely piloted it over the third reading. The House of Lords having rejected the Bill for Abolition of Purchase, Mr. Gladstone effected his object by an unprecedented use of the Royal Prerogative. This was the subject of a vote of censure by the House of Lords, and gave Lord Salisbury a congenial opportunity of indulging his caustic vein. The University Tests Bill naturally engaged much attention from him; and when war broke out between France and Germany, Lord Salisbury moved that our obligations to maintain the integrity of Holland and Belgium should be laid on the table, lest, tainted by an apathy bred of mingled ignorance and unconcern, Great Britain should allow the pitiful drama of Schleswig-Holstein to be re-enacted, *mutatis mutandis*. Indian finance was a constant object of Lord Salisbury's solicitude.

The Session of 1872 produced two well-known Bills; one—the Ballot Act, and the other—the Licensing Act.

The policy of the Liberal Government with respect to the South African Colonies called down the vials of Lord Salisbury's wrath upon them; but the Ministry, possessing to an inordinate degree that snug self-complacency, ignored the warning, and proceeded with the disastrous policy which culminated in the abject surrender to the Boers.

In 1871 and 1872 the Marquess of Salisbury was, with Lord Cairns, engaged in the onerous task of extricating the affairs of the London, Chatham, and Dover Railway Company from the confusion into which they had fallen. The arbitrators were so successful in this, that in eighteen months they had unravelled and subsequently satisfactorily arranged the details of various securities and properties valued at over £17,000,000. On July 21st the Duke of St. Albans was brought to book in the House of Lords for unconstitutional language which he had used at a provincial banquet. The words used implied that the Queen was a partizan of the Liberal Party. The Duke of Richmond questioned the Duke of St. Albans on the subject, and after the latter had replied by a lame attempt at justification, the Marquess of Salisbury completely and effectively disposed of the attempt at defence which the Duke of St. Albans had made.

The Liberal Government had been gradually discrediting themselves with the nation; they had been defeated in the House, and when the bye-elections resulted in gains to the Conservative Party, Mr. Gladstone's petulance could brook it no longer, and in a fit of temper he dissolved Parliament in January, 1874.   In his address Mr. Gladstone promised to abolish the Income Tax—but all in vain ; the whole run of the elections was in favour of the Conservative Party, and at the conclusion of the polling there resulted a majority of fifty in favour of that party.

Mr. Gladstone resigned office at once, and on February 18, 1874, Mr. Disraeli was summoned to the Royal presence, and received a command to form a new Ministry.

The Conservative Cabinet was constituted as follows :—

First Lord of the Treasury ...	Mr. Disraeli.
Lord Chancellor	Lord Cairns.
Lord President of the Council ...	The Duke of Richmond.
Lord Privy Seal	The Earl of Malmesbury.
Foreign Secretary	The Earl of Derby.
Secretary for India	The Marquess of Salisbury.
Colonial Secretary	The Earl of Carnarvon.
Secretary for War	Mr. Gathorne Hardy.
Home Department	Mr. R. A. Cross.
First Lord of the Admiralty ...	Mr. Ward Hunt.
Chancellor of the Exchequer ...	Sir Stafford Northcote.
Postmaster-General	Lord John Manners.

CHAPTER VI.

THE INDIAN FAMINE—THE EASTERN QUESTION—CONFERENCE AT CONSTANTI-
NOPLE—WAR WITH RUSSIA AND TURKEY—THE BERLIN TREATY—
UNIVERSITY REFORM—TROUBLES IN SOUTH AFRICA—GENERAL ELECTION,
1880—DEATH OF LORD BEACONSFIELD.

LORD SALISBURY had, on taking office, to face one of the gravest
administrative responsibilities which has ever fallen to an Indian
Secretary—the question of a famine in such a densely populated
country as India. In addition, the situation was complicated by the
Lieutenant-Governor of Bengal and the Viceroy each having diametrically opposed plans for relief. Sir George Campbell proposed to
prohibit the exportation of rice, and Lord Northbrook proposed to
import rice.

Sir George Campbell's plan was the popular one, and Lord Northbrook was a Liberal, but the Marquess of Salisbury at once and
emphatically endorsed the plan of his political opponent, and by a
series of well-timed and vigorous steps the disaster was minimized.

In fact, India has known no period in which she has made greater
progress, or enjoyed greater prosperity, than when the Marquess of
Salisbury has been at the Indian Office or at Downing Street.

Mr. Disraeli's Cabinet did not wantonly pull down some old-time
historical institution, nor did they build up any new jerry-built house
with shoddy and veneer; neither did they, like Sir Pertinax, " boo
an' boo " to every foreign power : and on this account the crochet-
mongers have pointed to the Session of 1874–80 as a barren one, but it
was by no means so. A qualified practitioner who is called in to a
patient on whom some clumsy village blacksmith has been practising
surgery, has enough to do to save his patient's life and then to restore
his shattered frame to health, without performing useless *ad captandum*
amputations for the delectation of the ignorant. This was the case
in 1874 when Mr. Disraeli took office ; all the great (?) measures of
the preceding Government were incomplete, each had to be amended,

and foreign countries had to be assured that Great Britain was still a first-class Power, with a definite foreign policy.

The Public Worship Act was the *magnum opus* of 1874, but is now only remembered for the passage of arms between two principal members of the Cabinet, the Premier and Lord Salisbury, who took opposite sides with regard to the measure. The Opposition attempted to make some capital out of the affair; the incident, however, resulted in the two persons immediately concerned becoming better friends than ever.

Mr. Gladstone completed in the beginning of 1875 the abdication of which he had given notice in 1874. Like a child who doesn't get all his own way, he said, "I won't play," and until the Eastern Question cropped up occupied his time in denying the possibility of any one else, even the Pope, being infallible, in wielding the axe, which is doubtless good training for "throwing the hatchet," and trying to render Homer more famous by connecting his own name with that of the poor heathen.

The Eastern Question was once more brought to the fore, and a European war almost brought about by a small insurrection in Herzegovina, which, not being promptly suppressed at its outset, gradually grew and grew till at last it culminated in the Russo-Turkish War. Before matters had gone very far the Powers presented to the Porte an identical Note, known as the Andrassy Note, pointing out that certain reforms were necessary. The Porte was most polite, but that was all. Finding no result accrued from the Andrassy Note, Russia, Prussia, and Austria drew up the Berlin Memorandum, which the English Cabinet very properly refused to join in. Then followed the "atrocity agitation," which gave Mr. Gladstone an opportunity to vent his spleen on the unspeakable Turk.

In June, 1876, Servia and Montenegro declared war against Turkey, who, though the smaller States were assisted by Russia, gradually got the mastery. Then came the proposition for a Conference from Lord Derby. The Powers assented to it. The Conference was to be held at Constantinople, and Lord Salisbury and Sir Henry Elliot were deputed to attend it.

Here again his administrative ability showed itself. On his way to Constantinople he conferred with the various Foreign Ministers at Paris, Berlin, Vienna, and Rome. Several schemes were proposed, but Lord Salisbury ultimately secured the adoption of the British one, viz., Servia and Montenegro to be placed *in statu quo*—Bosnia and Herzegovina to be locally autonomous—Turkey to give security for the preservation of law and order in Bulgaria, and also for its good administration. But his efforts were in vain as far as the Porte was concerned, as it obstinately refused to listen to the advice of the Conference. The Marquess of Salisbury, therefore, in January, 1877, returned to England. Sir Henry Elliot was recalled, and Mr. Layard took his place. Mr. Gladstone attacked Sir Henry Elliot for perverting the facts about atrocities. The Government defended Sir Henry, whom they stated to be an upright and honourable public servant, and that his recall was necessitated from the fact that the Government intended to uphold Lord Salisbury's policy, and express strong disapproval of the Turkish policy, and this could not be done so well by one who had strong Turkish sympathies.

In April, 1877, Russia declared war against Turkey. After varying fortunes, the Russians arrived at the gates of Constantinople in the beginning of 1878. The Government acted promptly. The fleet was ordered up the Dardanelles, and the Chancellor of the Exchequer demanded a credit of £6,000,000. Lord Carnarvon resigned, fearing that the Government were rushing into war. Then came the news of the Treaty of San Stefano. Lord Beaconsfield (Mr. Disraeli had been created Earl of Beaconsfield on August 12, 1876) announced that Russia should have no separate treaty with Turkey, and that what was done must be done by a European Congress. The Government called out the reserves, and summoned a contingent of Sepoys to Europe. Lord Derby, now thoroughly unnerved, resigned at once. Lord Salisbury took the post as Foreign Secretary at once, and on the 1st of April issued his famous circular, and June the 13th saw the Earl of Beaconsfield and the Marquis of Salisbury seated in the Radziwill Palace as the representatives of Great Britain at the Congress of Berlin. How truly and how successfully they championed the interests of England subsequent events have proved, and on their return to England bearing " Peace with honour," the two Ministers were invested with the Order of the Garter.

I have gone somewhat ahead, and it is necessary to go back somewhat; for, despite his journey to Constantinople and his interest in the Eastern Question, the Marquess of Salisbury by no means neglected his duties at the Indian Office. In 1875 Lord Salisbury promoted the Indian Legislation Act, and had to deal with the difficult question concerning the Guikwar of Baroda. Troubles also arose with respect to Burmah, and the Viceroy of India and the Marquess of Salisbury had a serious misunderstanding over a constitutional question, which resulted in the resignation of Lord Northbrook (the Viceroy), and the complete justification of Lord Salisbury's action in the matter. On February 24, 1876, the Marquess of Salisbury showed that in the midst of his multifarious duties he had not forgotten his *alma mater*, for on that date he introduced in the House of Lords a Bill dealing with the question of University Reform. The Bill only dealt with the University of Oxford, of which Lord Salisbury was Chancellor, but it was understood that a similar Bill dealing with Cambridge was soon to follow. The two Bills reached the second reading, but were unfortunately included in the massacre of the innocents; in 1877, however, the two Bills, consolidated into one, passed both Houses.

In 1877 another famine occurred in India, but, profiting by former experiences, the danger was efficiently coped with.

No sooner were the difficulties in the East of Europe smoothed over than others began to arise farther East. Russia had been intriguing with Afghanistan, and as a consequence the Ameer of that country refused to receive a Mission from England, though a Russian Embassy had but a short time previously been received with pomp and acclamation. No greater insult could be conceived than this ; the Government therefore called upon the Ameer to make reparation for the insult, otherwise war would be declared. The Ameer refused and the Afghan War began. The war resulted in the dethronement of Shere Ali and the substitution of his son, Yakoob Khan. As in the debate on this war the Marquess of Salisbury was charged with "disingenuousness," it would perhaps be as well to give his reply.

Before doing this we must go back to the 15th of June, 1877, when the Duke of Argyll asked the Secretary for India (the Marquess of Salisbury) for information with regard to.

1st. Whether the Government of India had determined upon a complete change of policy, and had resolved to insist on the Ameer receiving a Resident British Envoy at his Court :

2nd. Whether a particular officer had been appointed or was likely to be appointed—one whom he (the Duke of Argyll) knew to be a man of great ability and energy, and who on that very account would be regarded by so jealous a personage as the Ameer with all the greater suspicion :

3rd. Whether this change of policy had been backed up by the movement of a considerable body of troops under circumstances not easily understood, but which seemed to point to aggression on the North-West frontier :

4th. Whether a bridge of boats had been prepared on the Indus : and

5th. Whether, alarmed by diplomatic demands and military arrangements, the mind of the Ameer was thoroughly unsettled ; and whether he was in a state of agitation and anger, and was collecting troops to resist aggression and perhaps to make an aggressive movement upon India.

To these questions Lord Salisbury replied :—

" With respect to the information asked for by the noble Duke, I can hardly give him much positive knowledge, but I think I can give him some negative information. He has derived from the sources open to him the following statement, as I understood him : that we had tried to force an Envoy on the Ameer at Cabul—that we had selected for that purpose Sir Lewis Pelly, whose vigour of mind and action might possibly inspire apprehension in the councils of a native prince—that we had supported this demand by a large assemblage of troops on the North-Western frontier, and that we were preparing boats on the Indus. Now we have not tried to force an Envoy upon the Ameer at Cabul. We have not suggested Sir Lewis Pelly as an Envoy to Cabul—the troops were assembled on the North-Western frontier without the slightest reference to any such demand ; and with regard to the boats on the Indus, I never heard of them until to-day. Our relations with the Ameer of Cabul have undergone no material change since last year. I do not believe that he is worse disposed towards us than hitherto, or that his feelings are in any way embittered towards the British Government. I cannot follow the noble Duke into a description of his character, nor can I enter upon that very thorny question, how far the great movements of the principal European Powers are connected with the events to which he refers. The matter is one deserving serious attention, and when the occasion arises it will call for proper precautions. There is no doubt that the contest between Russia and Turkey has produced among the nations bordering on India a certain recrudescence of Mussulman feeling which I do not think will issue in any action attended with the slightest danger to our Indian Empire, but which may very well cause vigilance and care on the part of the British Government, and may induce those who are always on the look out for news in India to imagine that something stronger and more definite has occured than has really happened. If it is necessary to reopen the Conference, it will be done under better auspices. I only wish emphatically to repeat that none of those suspicions of aggression on the part of the English Government have any true foundation ; that our desire in the future, as it has been in the past, is to respect the Afghan Ruler, and to maintain as far as we can the integrity of his dominions.   There is no ground for any of the apprehensions to which the noble Duke has referred, or for suspicions which are too absurd to be seriously entertained.   The affairs of the Frontier are maintaining a peaceful aspect, with the exception of a little trouble with a local tribe—the Afreedees.   We have also maintained our relations with Khelat, and the papers we have laid on the table will explain what has occurred.   But there is no reason for any apprehension of any change of policy or of disturbance in our Indian Empire."

On the 5th of December, 1878, Earl Granville, having accused the Marquess of Salisbury of " disingenuousness " in the matter of his reply to the Duke of Argyll, the Marquess at once rose and said :—

" I do not wish to detain your Lordships on this personal matter, but the accusation which the noble Earl made against me was substantially this—that being questioned by the Duke of Argyll, I misled the House as to the real state of the case.   The noble Earl quoted my words in justification of that charge.   He began by saying that my words would indicate what the nature of the Duke of Argyll's question had been.   I regret that he did not quote the actual question of the Duke of Argyll.   When a legal opinion is produced, it is usual to give the question on which the legal opinion was founded.   When the *dictum* of a judge is quoted, it is a matter of ordinary practice to ask what was the precise nature of the case to. which the *dictum* refers. Words taken by themselves are often misleading, instead of giving information.   As I understand the charge of the noble Earl, it is that at a time when I knew that Sir Lewis Pelly had been commissioned to go to Cabul I denied that any Envoy had been sent to Cabul at all. Now, my lords, it is necessary to read the question of the Duke of Argyll to which I replied. What he said is spread over a speech of considerable length. I will not read many passages, but I will select some of them. They go to show that what the Duke of Argyll asked was as to whether it was true that I had forced on the Ameer of Cabul a Resident at his Court. The Duke of Argyll said : ' No doubt it would be very convenient to have a Resident at Cabul, if you could get a man for the place, and that he was received with cordiality, but it was notorious for a long time past that the present Ameer had set his face against having such an officer in his Court. . . . Rumour said that the Government of India had determined upon a change of policy, and had resolved to insist on the Ameer having a residentBritish Envoy at the Court.'

" Well, my Lords, the noble Earl said parenthetically, in the course of his remarks, that I should not attempt to explain the statement by asserting that what we had deliberately attempted to do was to attempt to induce the Ameer to receive resident Envoys at other places besides Cabul. I dare say when the noble Earl made that observation, he thought it was unimportant whether the Ameer received an Envoy at Cabul or Herat. But the difference is essential. Her Majesty's Government had been impressed with the opinion that to ask the Ameer to receive an Envoy at Cabul would be not only idle, but unwise, because of the turbulent and revengeful character of the population, which would render the residence of the Envoy dangerous. Moreover, there is no doubt that a resident at Cabul would have such powers of interfering in the internal government of Afghanistan, and of overshadowing the dignity of the Prince himself, that such a proposal would have very naturally raised objections in the mind of the Ameer—objections which it was the desire of Her Majesty's Government to avoid raising. We did not want to interfere in the internal government of Afghanistan, or to overshadow the authority of the Ameer. What we wanted was to have officers on the frontiers, who might see something of what was going on within them and beyond them—I need hardly explain to the .House why we should wish to know what was going on in Afghanistan. It is sufficient to say that the year before Khiva had been occupied—without going further I am sure the House will understand why we desired to know what was going on in Turkestan and in the Ameer's territories, without having any intention whatever of interfering in the internal government of Afghanistan, or overshadowing the Ameer in his own court. I dwell upon this point to show that the difference between asking for an Agent at Herat and at Cabul is immense. It was a distinction upon which the Ameer insisted all along. We have a curious account in Lord Lytton's letters in 1877, derived from officers who saw the Ameer at Umballa. A considerable number of them represented that they knew from personal knowledge that while the Ameer was willing to admit an Agent at Herat or on his frontiers, he would not admit one at Cabul.

"We were exceedingly careful to avoid making this particular demand to which the Ameer was certain to object. My first instructions to Lord Northbrook were, that he should take measures for obtaining the assent of the Ameer to the establishment of a British Envoy at Herat, but I did not suggest any similar step with regard to Cabul. Lord Lytton, when he came to propose the terms on which the negotiations should be conducted, was careful to make a similar distinction. He says in Article 5 of the Treaty, he proposed that for the protection of the Afghan Frontier, British Agents should reside at Herat, and at such other places as might be agreed upon by the contracting Powers; but farther on the Treaty says, that unless and until it is otherwise agreed, a Native Agent only should reside at Cabul. With this understanding, I think your Lordships will see that my reply to the Duke of Argyll was absolutely correct. I had first to inform him that I could not give him any positive knowledge. The circumstances at the time were difficult and critical in the extreme. Russia was in arms; great irritation prevailed; no one knew whether the war would not spread much farther than its original area; and whatever the policy of Her Majesty's Government might be, and whatever duties it might be called on to perform, this, at least, was our duty—not to bias in any way the policy of the country, nor to add to its difficulties and dangers by any imprudent language of our own. It was, therefore, our duty not to say much of that which I say now, and which is said in the papers before the House. Consequently, I told the Duke of Argyll that I could not give him much positive information, but that I could give him some negative information. The negative information was this—that we had not tried to force an

Envoy on the Ameer at Cabul, and that we had not suggested Sir
Lewis Pelly as an Envoy at Cabul.   Now I want to know why the
noble Earl opposite (Earl Granville) insinuates that I said anything
contrary to the most perfect truth in the reply I made to the Duke of
Argyll.   The noble Earl who sits on the cross-benches (Earl Grey)
talked of my having stated that there had been no change of policy as
regards Afghanistan.   I must charitably suppose that the noble Earl
spoke without having taken the trouble to read the speech to which
he referred.   There is no such statement in that speech.   The noble
Earl remarked that I said that our relations with the Ameer had
undergone no material change since last year, and that the Ameer's
feelings towards the British Government were not more embittered
than they had been.   Now, if I had said that his feelings were not
more embittered towards us than they had been when Lord Mayo met
him at Umballa, there might be a considerable doubt as to the accuracy
of that statement.   His feelings are undoubtedly a matter of some
mystery : but I have little doubt that they have gone on deteriorating
progressively against us from the time when Sir John Lawrence came
to the unfortunate resolution not to take what has been called the
honest double dealing policy with regard to the candidates for the
throne of Afghanistan.   I have no doubt they became worse and
worse.   There was a slight improvement, however, during the Viceroyalty of Lord Mayo ; but during the Viceroyalty of Lord Northbrook
there were several circumstances which caused them to become worse
and worse.   There was that unfortunate arbitration at Seistan, with
which the Ameer was profoundly dissatisfied ; and which only added
one to the list of those arbitrations which have not precisely produced
that perfect good feeling which the devisers of the system hoped for.
Then there was an act which reflects great credit on Lord Northbrook,
who was then Viceroy, but which much displeased the Ameer.   That
was Lord Northbrook's interposition to save the son of the Ameer,
Yakoob Khan, from suffering the worst results of one of the most
atrocious acts of perfidy which ever an Afghan ruler ever committed.
What I desired to express, and what was a distinct and a true answer
to all the questions of the Duke of Argyll was, that the policy which
led to the Conference at Peshawur had not made an unfavourable
difference in the dispositions of the Ameer—his feelings were already
as hostile to us as they could well be.   I can only go to the official

documents.   The noble Earl says—what is perfectly true—that I received the dispatch of Lord Lytton about a week before I made that answer in the House.   Well, what are we to take as proof of the Ameer's relations towards us?   I will first take the Ameer's own account.   I find this in Lord Lytton's dispatch—

"'So completely had the whole movement collapsed before we closed the Conference at Peshawur, that the first step taken by the Ameer, immediately after that event, was to send messengers to the authorities and population of Candahar, informing them that the Jehad project was abandoned, requesting them to do all in their power to allay the religious excitement he had till then been endeavouring to arouse, and adding that his relations with the British Government were eminently satisfactory.'

"With that statement in my hands, I could not say in this House that our relations with the Ameer were unsatisfactory.   Lord Lytton, in the meanwhile, said—

"'We see no reason to anticipate any act of aggression on the part of the present Ameer;' and he added, 'Our relations with him are still such as we might commonly maintain with the Chiefs of neighbouring and friendly countries.'   That is exactly the position which it was the ambition of Lord Lawrence, and, subsequently, of Lord Northbrook, to maintain.   What was my own official estimate some three months later of the state of things?   I said we had been engaged in negotiations, the object of which was not to maintain our relations with the Ameer unchanged, but to make them more friendly than they had been.   He refused our advances, and when I spoke in the House I knew that those advances had been refused.   My statement, therefore, was in all its parts strictly in accordance with facts."

On the 10th idem, the Marquess of Bath having reiterated the accusation, the Marquess of Salisbury gave it the further emphatic denial quoted below:—

"The noble Marquess below the gangway (the Marquess of Bath) has addressed some reproaches to me.   He was in some difficulty, naturally, to find a reason for the vote he is about to give, and he gave as his reason that I had used some language last year which he was pleased to say was not accurate.   My Lords, I prefer resignedly abandoning my character in the eyes of the noble Marquess to keeping your Lordships out of bed ; therefore, I shall not go into the matter, which I dealt with sufficiently on a previous occasion. I will merely say that the Duke of Argyll asked me certain questions which I thought it proper and expedient should be answered. He asked me whether certain troops were assembled to force a Resident upon the Ameer; he spoke of a bridge of boats erected on the Indus to facilitate operations: he wished to know whether there was any departure from a policy which had been adopted by many Indian statesmen, and whether any attempt was being made to force on the Ameer a Resident at the Court of Cabul—' Resident at the Court of a Native Prince ' being an expression whose significance is well understood in India. To that question I gave a negative answer. He asked me for positive information. I told him I could not give positive information; and because, under these circumstances, noble Lords opposite appear to have mis-understood what I intended to say, the noble Marquess and others are pleased to accuse me of disingenuousness. I imagined every one in this House knew there were many subjects on which the mouth of a Minister of the Crown is sealed, and they cannot always explain fully what their policy is. If I had explained fully what our policy then was, I must have explained the reasons on which it was founded: I must have depicted the Ameer as he had been depicted to me, as a faithless, treacherous, intriguing man, whose loyalty we had vainly attempted to secure. The noble Marquess has forgotten that anything said here by a Minister of the Crown is said not merely to this House of Lords and the English people, but to the whole world—to the Czar of Russia, to the Shah of Persia, and to the Ameer of Afghanistan, and if you insist that no answer shall be given except such as contains a complete revelation of the policy of the Government, the only inference I draw is, that in the future no answer at all can be given to questions of that kind."

As a result of the South African policy inaugurated by Mr. Gladstone's Ministry, some difficulty was experienced at the close of 1878 with regard to the Zulus, which ultimately led to the Zulu War. This war, marked by the defeat and slaughter of our troops at Isandhlwana, dragged on till July, 1880; but before that time England had seen some remarkable changes.

That commercial depression from which we are even now suffering, though in a less degree, had begun to make itself severely felt in the beginning of 1879, and was increasing in intensity towards the close of that year. This was not lost sight of by the Opposition, who, not being able to successfully attack the foreign policy of the Government on its own merits, assured the people that the depression at home was the price they, the people, had to pay for success abroad. This proved a most taking argument, and by it the Liberals managed to undermine the popularity of the Government.

The Opposition had by this time both recovered from their defeat and become once more united. Then came the celebrated Midlothian campaign.

At length in March, 1880, Parliament was dissolved,. and the elections began. The Ballot then proved to be what Lord Salisbury had so aptly described it, " a *régime* of surprises." Worn out by the continued depression in trade, and deceived by the plausible proffers of the Liberals, the people made a grand *volte-face*. A huge Liberal wave swept over the country, effacing the Conservative majority, and giving the Liberals an even larger majority than their opponents had had.

Lord Beaconsfield resigned, and after *pro formâ* negotiations with Lord Hartington and Lord Granville, Mr. Gladstone was ordered to form a Ministry.

The Liberal Government began well. ' The Burials Bill and the Ground Game Act were the sops to the Dissenters and the farmers respectively ; then the Irish difficulty made legislation impossible.

Mr. Forster, the Secretary for Ireland, had brought in a Compensation for Disturbance Bill, which had been rejected by the Lords by a majority of 241. This, as may be imagined, did not produce a soothing effect on the Irish Party, and as a consequence little more was done by Parliament in 1880.

Parliament met again on January 7, 1881. The Ministry, unable to effect legislation at home, began discrediting the nation abroad by first of all truckling to Russia by retreating from Afghanistan, and secondly by making an abject surrender to the petty Boer Republic.

Lord Salisbury protested in most vigorous language against each, but it was useless appealing to the sordid Liberal mind on a question of national honour. Lord Beaconsfield also spoke against the Afghan policy of the Government, and spoke for the last time, for on the 19th of April Benjamin Disraeli, Earl of Beaconsfield, died.

CHAPTER VII.

LORD SALISBURY LEADER OF THE CONSERVATIVE PARTY—THE IRISH LAND
    BILL—THE PHŒNIX PARK MURDERS—THE BOMBARDMENT OF ALEX-
    ANDRIA—VARIOUS ACTS OF PARLIAMENT—THE SESSION OF 1883—
    THE COUNTY FRANCHISE BILL.

THE death of the Earl of Beaconsfield marks the third epoch in the
political life of the Marquess of Salisbury. Had not Lord Beaconsfield died, it is probable that the Marquess would not have so strongly
impressed his individuality on the politics of the last few years as he
has done. Never rising, like Mr. Gladstone, to the level of a fetish,
he has, from his consistency, been perhaps a stronger factor in political
life than his opponent.

On May 9, 1881, the Marquess of Salisbury was unanimously
elected the leader of the Conservative party in the House of Lords in
succession to the Earl of Beaconsfield.

His first duties in his new position were of a very difficult nature,
involving the question of the respective duties of the House of Lords
and the House of Commons.

Under another leader these difficulties would have been intensified,
but as Lord Salisbury (as I quoted previously) had already formulated
his views on the subject, the House of Lords, acting under his guid-
ance, could not be accused of acting otherwise than consistently and
conscientiously.

On April 7th, Mr. Gladstone had introduced his Irish Land Bill
in the House of Commons, and by July 29th it had reached the third
reading in that House. It then reached the Upper House, where it
was given a second reading. Before the Bill was passed, however, a
number of amendments were made by the Lords, which were fiercely
opposed by the extreme members of the House of Commons. After
these amendments had been twice before the Lower House a compromise was arranged.

In October the Government arrested Messrs. Parnell, Sexton,

O'Kelly, Dillon, O'Brien, and Quinn; but in the following April, owing to the famous Kilmainham Treaty, they were released.

On May 6th Lord Frederick Cavendish and Mr. Burke were murdered in Phœnix Park, Dublin.

Mr. Trevelyan became Irish Secretary, and on July 14th a Coercion Bill of exceptional severity was passed.

So much for the policy of conciliation.

The Coercion Act, I should mention, was not allowed to pass without being thoroughly overhauled by the House of Lords, and another standstill between the two Houses was the result. Another compromise, however, brought the difficulty to an end.

England, it was thought, would be sure to favour an " oppressed nationality ; " and, secure in this belief, Arabi Pacha fomented an insurrection in Egypt. The bombardment of Alexandria followed on July 11th, and this again was followed, with the usual haste of a Liberal Government, in September by the dispatch of an expedition to Egypt.

Who, that in 1878 had listened to the speeches of Mr. Gladstone against the policy of Lord Beaconsfield, and in particular against three acts connected therewith, viz., the calling out of the reserves, the summoning of Sepoys from India, and the acquisition of Cyprus, would believe that four years later Mr. Gladstone himself would repeat the first two, and make use of Cyprus as a base of operations ! But it has been truly said that Liberal Governments have a "sliding-scale of insolence." It was wrong to do these things when a great Power like Russia was concerned, but with respect to a petty band of insurgents in a country like Egypt anything was lawful.

The autumn Session of 1882 was occupied with the passing of the Procedure Bills, Lord Cairns' Settled Estates Act, and the Married Women's Property Act.

In November, at Edinburgh, Lord Salisbury made a spirited speech, picturing what Mr. Gladstone would have said had a Conservative Ministry done what the Liberal Ministry had done in Egypt.

At the opening of Parliament in February, 1883, the Marquess made a studied speech in the debate on the Address. He said that the proposer of the Address " said that the Speech was one which must give great satisfaction to the House to hear. However that may be, I doubt whether it is one that gave great satisfaction to its

authors to compose. It gives me the impression of an ordeal by fir e
A number of burning questions lie about—matters of the deepest
interest to the world—and the Speech moves about among the red-
hot plough-shares with delicate steps, scarcely touching one of them,
and certainly not allowing to remain upon its surface the slightest
imprint of their contact." He went on to taunt the Government with
want of agreement. The Secretary of State for the Colonies had said
that a million or two a year spent on emigration in Ireland would
prove a panacea—then the Marquis of Hartington stepped forward
and denied it. Mr. Herbert Gladstone had said he was in favour of
Home Rule—Mr. Ashley would not grant Home Rule; "while Mr.
Courtney pronounced a perfectly Pindaric eulogium on the advantages of anarchy." Mr. Chamberlain says, "As long as Ireland is
without any institution of local government worthy of the name, so
long the seeds of discontent and disloyalty will remain, only to burst
forth into luxurious growth at the first favourable season." As to
Mr. Gladstone, "his constituents in Midlothian have, to their great
grief, failed to receive a defence of his policy," but having "abandoned the senate and the platform," Mr. Gladstone has "taken refuge
behind the tea-table," and there he states—"The curse of Ireland is
centralization. What I hope and desire, what I labour for and have
at heart, is to decentralize authority there. We have disestablished the
Church, and have relieved the tenant class of many grievances, and are
now going to produce a state of things which will make the humblest
Irishman realize that he is a governing agency, and that is to be
carried on for him and by him." " I," added Lord Salisbury, "do
not like the idea of the humblest Irishman as a governing agency.
What does Lord Hartington say? He says, 'It is supposed by some
that by changes in the system of local self-government we can restore
contentment to the country. It would be madness, in my opinion, to
give Ireland more extended self-government, unless we receive from
the Irish people some assurance that this boon would not be used for
the purpose of agitation.' Now it is not for me to reconcile these
divergent opinions. What I do wish to press upon the House, and
upon Her Majesty's Government, is that this is no mere question of
inconsistency. It is a question whether, in a crisis of singular
importance in Irish history, the Government have presented to the
Irish people a plain and distinct policy in which they are all agreed;

or whether, by their expressed disagreement, they are not encouraging the Irish people to further efforts in agitation."

The only things of which the Liberals can boast during this year (1883), are the proposal to lend M. Lesseps £8,000,000 at 3 per cent. in order that he might make a second Suez Canal, the Bankruptcy Act, and allowing the insurrection under the " Madhi" to continue uncontrolled.

The Marquess of Salisbury is credited with an article in the November number of *The Quarterly Review*, entitled " Disintegration." It is a strong and almost a prophetic paper, and the following excerpt is especially worthy of quotation:

" This is not the Parliamentary Government under which the nation lived a century ago, when the position of a strong Minister was secure from the sudden revulsions of feeling in the House of Commons; but, on the other hand, when his action was effectively controlled by the still vigorous power of the aristocracy and of the Crown.

" Again, it is a popular impression that our existing system has the sanction of the experience of the Great Western Republic, and that American institutions are practically the same as ours, differing only in that they are a little more democratic.

" The resemblance is entirely superficial. The elements of instability and insecurity, which are so rife in our institutions as they at present practically stand, have been wisely excluded from the American system. Our House of Commons has come into its position, as it were, by accident. It is like the junior member of a great mercantile firm, who has suddenly become all powerful, not in pursuance of any articles of the partnership, but simply because the senior partners have fallen into poor health, and have retired. No provision was made in the articles to meet such a contingency; and his power is absolutely unrestricted. The House of Representatives at Washington is in a very different position. The Constitution of the United States was framed by men, deeply mistaken, as we think, in that they were hostile to monarchy, but yet fully sensible of the dangers that attended the democracy they chose; and it was with these dangers fully in their view that they limited the functions and counterpoised the power of the supreme assemblies they set up. Both in America and England the popular vote indirectly chooses the party from which the Ministers are to be drawn, in the one case by the election of a President, in the other by the election of a House of Commons; but the tenure of the Ministers is very different. In America they practically hold during the four years' Presidential term; they do not sit in Congress, and cannot be displaced by any action of Congress short of an impeachment. The difference between a secure and precarious tenure affects the mind of the politician as much as that of the agriculturist; and, accordingly, American Ministers do not find it necessary to recommend legislative measures with an eye chiefly to the party interests of the moment, and to the composition of their majority from day to day. One of the results of this condition of things is the comparative absence of a class of legislation with which in England we are too familiar. No group of members has the power of intimating to a Minister, ' Unless this or that measure on which we have set our hearts is supported by the Government, they must not count on our support in the next critical division.' Personal purity is unhappily low in American politics; and unless they are maligned, the lesser bribery, the bribery of individuals, frequently takes place. But the greater bribery, the bribery by legislation, the bribery of classes strong in political power at the cost of those who are weak— this kind of corruption is comparatively unknown."

In the spring of 1884 the Ministry led off with the Ilbert Bill fiasco, and then followed with the Franchise Bill.

This Bill was introduced in the Commons by Mr. Gladstone on Feb. 28th, and was met by an amendment by Lord John Manners that the Bill should not be proceeded with until the Government scheme of Redistribution of Seats was before the House. The Amendment was, however, defeated by 340 to 210, and after a severe battle in Committee, the Bill ultimately reached the Upper House. There it was met on the second reading by an amendment moved by Lord Cairns, similar to Lord John Manners' amendment in the Commons, and this was carried by 205 to 146. Two days afterwards Mr. Gladstone, "*aut Cæsar, aut nihil*," threatened an Autumn Session for the sole purpose of considering the same Bill. A motion was made in the House of Lords that the decision should be reconsidered, but the motion was promptly rejected and the Lords stood firm.

The Marquess of Salisbury's position throughout all this had been clear and well defined, and with regard to it he said that the Liberals admitted the necessity of a Redistribution Bill to accompany the Franchise Bill, and had promised to introduce one when the Franchise Bill was passed; he did not doubt their honour, but he did doubt their absolute ability to make good their promise. Events might arise which would put such a thing completely out of their power—and under such circumstances it was the best, and, in fact, the only possible, course to insist on the Redistribution Bill being produced while the Ministry had not only the will but the power.

When the Autumn Session commenced, the Franchise Bill was re-introduced into the Commons and again passed; it went up to the Lords and was read a first time—but four days afterwards Mr. Gladstone surrendered his position. Not only were the Lords to have their way, but the Redistribution Bill was to be approved of by Lord Salisbury. The Redistribution Bill was accordingly drawn up to the satisfaction of both parties, and it having been passed in the House of Commons, the House of Lords allowed the Franchise Bill to pass, and on the 5th of December, 1884, it received the Royal Assent.

CHAPTER VIII.

CONSTITUTIONALISM VERSUS LIBERALISM—THE HOUSING OF THE POOR—
RESIGNATION OF THE LIBERAL GOVERNMENT—LORD SALISBURY CALLED
TO OFFICE—GENERAL ELECTION, 1885—DEFEAT OF THE CONSERVA-
TIVES—LORD SALISBURY RESIGNS—THE GLADSTONE GOVERNMENT AND
HOME RULE—GENERAL ELECTION, 1886—DEFEAT OF THE LIBERALS
AND RESTITUTION OF LORD SALISBURY TO POWER—THE QUEEN'S VISIT
TO HATFIELD—CONCLUSION.

WHILE dealing with the question of Constitutionalism *versus* Liberalism, some words written by Lord Salisbury some eleven years
ago seem to be very appropriate.

"During the half-century of breathless change from which we are
apparently at last to have a respite, the position of these Moderate
Liberals has been very remarkable. While the torrent was passing,
they did not keep their feet better than other people. It has constantly happened to them to find themselves voting for that which
they had denounced; accepting logical conclusions, the fear of which
they had once derided as the ' hobgoblin argument;' proposing a first-
step as absolutely final, and then, some years later, proposing the second
as a necessary corollary of the first. A forecast in 1820 of their
proceedings during the following fifty years would have surprised no
one so much as themselves. Like John Gilpin, ' they little thought,
when they set out, of running such a rig.' But still they were
marked off from the bold companions by whose side they marched,
and whose ends they unwittingly served, by one strong distinction.
They genuinely believed in ' finality.' The particular reform in
hand was on each occasion desired by them for its own sake only—
as the exceptional remedy of an exceptional abuse—as a close of controversy—as a step towards political repose. They looked forward to
no vista of perpetual subversion. They did not imagine their party
to exist for the purpose of eternally devising new changes, and
agitating the public mind to carry them out. They would never have
recognized it as a reproach that their budget of reforms was exhausted,

and that they had no fresh institution to suggest for attack. It would never have occurred to them that it was the duty of a Liberal leader to collect his party, as if he were collecting moths and bats, by the exhibition of a 'blazing principle.' If they formed a party of change, it was because, in their judgment, great changes were required. It would not have entered into their philosophy that great changes ought to be proposed for the purpose of keeping the party of change together. The difference between the two sections is this: the moderate Liberals are Radicals *ad hoc;* the others are Radicals permanently. The one section mark trees to be cut down because they think a clearance is required; the others mark them because cutting down trees is their business; and when they have finished one job, they clamour against their leaders until they are conducted to another. It is the business of their leaders to find trees to be cut down. There lies the difficulty of the present moment. The Liberal leaders are in danger of being dethroned because they have not a fresh 'policy'—in other words, because they cannot find new and yet safe materials to gratify the destructive instincts of their followers. To the latter section of the party it is idle to talk of political repose. They believe what they call 'progress' is destruction. But to those Liberals who believe in finality, whose views of reform have a fixed horizon, the present is a juncture of supreme importance. The political aims of the party of movement are undergoing an entire revolution, which would have forced itself more prominently upon public attention if it had not been so far carried on with singularly little change of persons. The battle-field is changing, and the colours, and the objective point of the assailant's strategy: but a large proportion of the combatants remains the same. It is still the parson and the squire, and in the background the king and noble, who are the first objects of attack; though now there are associated with them a large class of employers of labour who used to be fighting on the other side, and who feel themselves in strange company. The assault is still conducted chiefly by poverty and philosophy; academical dreamers furnish to the movement its brains, and the Have-nots, who would gladly have without industry or thrift, supply its force. The Dissenters still contribute a large contingent; but, so far as they are not included in either of these two categories—so far as they are not hungry for endowment, or impatient of Christian belief—their alliance is traditional, depending more on habit than on present sympathy: and the same may be said of other classes of well-to-do auxiliaries, who are watching the motions of their allies with a not very friendly vigilance. But though there is in this country no very marked change in the composition of each host, the cause of battle is not the less rapidly changing."

On February 22, 1884, Lord Salisbury had moved for a Commission to inquire as to the housing of the poor, and made a practical speech, but the Government were too busy with ornamental statesmanship to heed such a low-class practical subject as that; so it had to stand over till Lord Salisbury was in power, which was not for long, for in June, 1885, the Liberal Government had "spent their majority," and were defeated on the Budget proposals. Mr. Gladstone thereupon resigned, and Lord Salisbury was ordered to form a Ministry.

This new Ministry could not reverse the policy with regard to Egypt that the late Government had pursued, so they contented themselves with remedying some of its former errors.

The Crimes Bill Lord Salisbury could not renew, because it would have an act of stultification on the part of Parliament to say by the Franchise Bill, "The people of Ireland are fit to receive an extended franchise," and by a Coercion Bill, "The people of Ireland cannot be ruled by the ordinary law."

The Government, however, passed the Act creating a Secretary for Scotland, and A Bill to Improve the Housing of the Working Classes, and an Irish Land Purchase Bill.

During the Autumn Recess the campaign, in view of the approaching dissolution of Parliament, was begun, and carried on with unceasing vigour up to the commencement of the polling. Amongst the almost numberless speeches delivered during this period, none attracted so much attention as that made by Lord Salisbury at Newport, on October 5th, 1884, from which I have taken the following extracts:—

"Our policy, I need not tell you, is to uphold the Turkish Empire whenever it can be genuinely and healthily upheld; but whenever its rule is proved by events to be inconsistent with the welfare of populations, then to strive to cherish and foster strong, self-sustaining nationalities who shall make a genuine and important contribution to the future freedom and independence of Europe. Our object, above all things, is peace, because if peace is broken, you never can be certain when armies are once in the field what the results of their efforts will lead to, and whether the results will be favourable to national growth or individual independence, and you never can be certain that the fate of small nations may not be sacrificed by the exigencies which military events may enable larger nations to acquire.

"I must again call your attention, before saying anything of the problems that lie before us, to the peculiar mode in which our opinions are dealt with by our opponents. Their plan is this, first to sketch out to you in brilliant and imaginative colours what they think the Conservative policy is. They prove to you what ought to be the Conservative policy, and then it naturally turns out· that they know nothing about the matter, and if the Conservatives take a very different view they declare that they are the basest of mankind, and abandon their own ideas for the sake of the sweets of office. Conservatives alone should be the exponents of Conservative opinion. I do not know anything so comical as a Radical trying to point out what a Conservative should be.

" Now, one of the subjects which, by common consent, must occupy the attention of the future Parliament, is one which our adversaries would persuade you that they only have the right to touch. I mean the subject of local government. Even Mr. Gladstone, in the long and dreary epistle which he, like an emperor of old, wrote from his retirement, even Mr. Gladstone is disposed to deny us the right of entertaining the question of local government. He is gracious to admit that I have expressed very strong opinions in its favour ; but he proceeds to point out that I have not the slightest influence over the opinions of my party, and that my influence must not be taken as any proof of what they really would think.

" I was very much struck by his warning, and I thought it better to provide myself with undoubted credentials. Therefore I did not venture to address you until I met my colleagues in the Cabinet.

" I do not know whether he thinks the Cabinet have any influence over the opinions of the Conservative party; but if the sixteen gentlemen who sit in the Cabinet are not to be expected to represent the opinions of the Conservative party, I will say that, without doubt and hesitation, and without a dissentient voice, they are strongly of opinion that large reforms in our local government are necessary, and in the direction of increasing powers to local governments are absolutely necessary.

"Bear in mind what true reform in local government means. I quite admit that the local authority should be popularly elected. But it does not mean that. You have not got at what you want when you have provided for the proper constitution of your local authority. You must provide it with sufficient power, and add to this power by diminishing the excessive and exaggerated powers which have been heaped upon the central authorities in London. That I claim to be a special Tory doctrine, which we have held through good report and evil report for many and many a generation.

"It has always been our contention that people in their own localities should govern themselves, and that the attempt to imitate the Continental plan by throwing every authority back upon the central power, though it might produce a more scientific and exact and more effective administration for the moment, will, when tested, be disastrous to all good government. It would not provide a government that was suited to the feelings and idiosyncrasies of a number of communities, and it would not teach the people to take that active nterest in their own government which is the only training that makes a man a true and worthy citizen.

"These are doctrines that we have held for a very long time. We urged them—that is to say, our fathers urged them—perhaps with undue persistency, and they opposed on that account the introduction of the New Poor Law. I am not blaming the New Poor Law. It was a necessary reform, in order to meet tremendous evils, but it did carry with it that spirit of centralization which has sunk deeply into our organization. It was opposed at the time by the Conservatives earnestly and strongly, and though I should be sorry to undo the beneficent action which may fairly be attributed to the New Poor Law, still I feel that the education of the country is so far advanced, the number of men capable of taking part in local government is so great, that the time has come when many of these powers now given to the Local Government Board and others in London ought to be given to the local authorities.

"There is one reform which I have very much at heart, and which I have urged so often that I do not think Mr. Chamberlain will say that I am trenching on his copyright in claiming it. It is that all men, in proportion to their ability, should contribute to the expenses of the local government. As you know, it is now defrayed by what are called rates, and they are not levied upon all men according to the amount of land or houses they may possess. They may possess very large resources, and yet escape altogether contributing to the administration of the local government. This is a disadvantage to their fellows. It is not merely an injustice to them; it does a great deal of harm. I have been sitting for two years upon a Commission in respect to the housing of the poor, which was appointed in answer to a motion which I moved in the House of Lords. I have a strong feeling that the unfair incidence of rates in many parts of the country is a question of material gravity. I hold it to be an indispensable part of any reform of your local government that it should include the sanction of this great principle—that all men should pay according to their ability.

" There is another matter of which you know something in this or in the neighbouring locality, and that is the burning question of Sunday closing. Sunday closing, looked at from a purely impartial point of view, presents these difficulties : that though in Scotland you have unanimity, in Ireland practical unanimity, and in Wales you have unanimity qualified by a certain amount of recent experience—and I am bound to admit that in Cornwall you have what appears to be unanimity—yet when you come to the strictly Teutonic portion of the community you have anything but unanimity.

" Looking at it from an impartial point of view, it is impossible not to see that the difficulties of a uniform system for the whole country are extreme ; and if we were not afraid of running against some anti-quated doctrines on the subject, we should adopt the simple principle of letting each locality decide for itself what it shall do in the matter. I venture to say that, as regards most of those who hear me, two words have rushed into their minds. They have said, ' He is pro-fessing local option.' The value of local option differs exactly according to the value of the thing about which the local option is to take place.

" I do not think local option is a bad thing when that matter upon which local option takes place is legitimate, but where local option is also used for a different process I have no kind of sympathy with it.

" It is proposed that localities shall have the power, where the number of non-thirsty souls exceeds the number of thirsty souls, that the non-thirsty souls shall have the power of saying that the thirsty souls shall have nothing at all to drink. That seems to be trenching upon the elementary liberties of mankind.

" If I like to drink beer, it is no reason that I should be prevented from taking it because my neighbour does not like it. If you sacrifice liberty on the matter of alcohol, you will eventually sacrifice it on more important matters also, and those advantages of civil and religious liberty for which we have fought hard will gradually be whittled away.

" I should therefore be inclined to trust the local authority with the settlement of this difficult question of Sunday closing, but always on one condition—that they should be trusted with the permanent settlement of it. That is to say, that if after two or three years' interval they did not like what they had done, they should be at liberty to retrace their steps. I do not understand any permanent views in this matter.

" Perhaps those who do not now like Sunday closing would alter their minds after some experience ; but I think the local authority should have the power to alter any resolution to which they had come— and for myself I should be prepared to go a step further, and give the local authority power over licenses to the extent which the magistrates exercise. I see no reason why they should exercise it less wisely and liberally than the magistrates, and I cannot blind myself to the fact that in some districts certain opinions have gained ground upon the bench which really disqualify magistrates from exercising a perfectly satisfactory judgment.

" But while I thus differ from the opinion of some I much respect, it is necessary to make this observation. . . .

" You will probably ask me, ' How far do you feel inclined to make this extension of local authority general ? How far, for instance, are you inclined to extend it to Ireland ? '

" This is a difficult question, I admit. Our first principle on which we have always gone is to extend to Ireland as far as we can all the institutions in this country. But I fully recognize that, in the case of local institutions especially, there is one element of consideration which in the state of Ireland you cannot leave out of mind.

" Local authorities are more exposed to the temptation of enabling the majority to be unjust to the minority when they obtain jurisdiction over a small area, than in the case where the authority derives its sanction and extends its jurisdiction over a wider area. It would be impossible to leave out of sight, in the extension of any such local authority to Ireland, the fact that the population is on several subjects deeply divided, and that it is the duty of every Government, on all matters of essential justice, to protect the minority against the majority.

" With respect to the larger organic questions connected with Ireland, I cannot say much though I can speak emphatically. I have nothing to say but that the traditions of the party to which we belong are on this subject clear and distinct, and you may rely upon it that our party will not depart from them. We look upon the integrity of the Empire as a matter more important than almost any other political consideration that you can imagine, and we could not regard with favour any proposal which directly or indirectly menaced that which is the first condition of England's position among the nations of the world.

" If I had spoken three days ago, I should not have said anything more upon Irish matters; but I observed in yesterday's papers a a remarkable speech from the Irish leader, in which he referred in so marked a way to the position of Austro-Hungary that I gathered that his words were intended to cover some kind of a new proposal, and that some notion of Imperial federation was floating in his mind. In speaking of Imperial federation as entirely apart from the Irish question, I wish to guard myself very carefully. I deem it to be one of the questions of the future.

" I believe the drawing nearer of the Colonies is the policy to which our English patriots must look who desire to give effect in the councils of the world to the real strength of the English nation. . . .

" Our opponents in their speeches say that we are opposed to passing measures for facilitating the transfer of land and cheapening it. You may be quite certain that there is more than a desire on our part to make the transfer of land and its sale cheap. . . .

" If the law says you shall have education, and they are unable to pay without enormous difficulty, then there is a reason why they should be assisted. I do not think we should make presents of large sums of public money to people perfectly competent to pay for the education of their children. As to religious education, which Mr.

Morley desires to get rid of, it is one of our most cherished privileges.

" You may hear (from the Radicals) a proposal for the disendowment of the Church of this country—a proposal fraught with frightful disaster to the nation, and more calamitous than any other change which has taken place. Our party is bound up with the maintenance of the established and endowed Church of the country."

The new Franchise and Redistribution Acts having come into operation on the 18th of November, 1885, Parliament was dissolved.

In the General Election which followed the Ministerialists gained a little, but the rout of the ex-Ministers was remarkable. The result, however, left the Government in a minority, there being 251 Conservatives against 333 Radicals and 86 Parnellites.

The new Parliament met on January 12, 1886, and on the 26th of the same month were defeated by a majority of 79 on Mr. Jesse Colling's Amendment to the Address. Lord Salisbury thereupon resigned, and Mr. Gladstone assumed the reins of office.

The Irish Question had now become the question of the hour. Many people had tried their hand at the Irish Secretaryship, and with varying success, but in the new Cabinet a new experiment was tried, and the very *beau ideal* of the class described a page or two back by Lord Salisbury as " academical dreamers who furnish to a movement its brains "—Mr. John Morley—became Chief Secretary for Ireland. On the 18th of February Lord Granville stated that the Government proposals with regard to Ireland would not be ready for six weeks. Lord Salisbury objected to the manner in which the Government was treating Parliament, but the Government persisted in silence. Not so some of its members. In March there was a stampede. Mr. Chamberlain resigned, Mr. Trevelyan resigned, and several minor luminaries preferred State to party, and left the Government.

On the 8th of April Mr. Gladstone introduced The Government of Ireland Bill. It was doomed from the first; but it lingered on till the 8th of June, and then Mr. Gladstone comprehended the measure of success of his Bill—it had converted a majority of over a hundred to a minority of thirty. Mr. Gladstone would not accept the verdict of Parliament; he appealed to the people, and the result was more staggering still—the new Parliament left him in a minority of 104.

Mr. Gladstone resigned, and Lord Salisbury had again to undertake the formation of a Ministry.

The new Parliament met in August, 1886, and in the debate on the Address Lord Salisbury gave a most lucid explanation of the Government policy, delivering himself with regard to foreign policy and Ireland as follows:—

" The policy of this country has been very clearly marked out for a considerable time, and it is our intention to adhere to the traditions that we have inherited. The integrity of the Turkish Empire, as defined by treaties, is of great importance in our judgment as it has been in the judgment of many statesmen in past times, of great importance to the peace of Europe, of great importance to the interests of this country. While desiring to do all we can to insure the welfare and the progress of the populations of those regions, we still hold by the integrity of the Turkish Empire as one of the conditions on which the present European system is based. We have every hope that in holding that view we shall, as in times past, have the support of our allies. They heartily approve the action initiated partly by ourselves, which was directed towards maintaining the integrity of the Turkish Empire, during the spring and summer of' this year. I still maintain the firm hope and belief that, by adhering steadily to the policy which has been the English policy for a great number of years, we shall contribute and contribute effectively to permanently maintain the peace of Europe. . . .

" We were returned with one mandate—to maintain the Union. We believe that we represent accurately the wishes of the people of this country, when we say that it is our duty to give our efforts, above everything else, to the restoration of social order and the maintenance of legal rights. Under the peculiar circumstances of Ireland the multiplication of freeholders will be a blessing and security for all who live in that country, and a solution of all the political questions with which we have had lately to deal to an extent which must make us anxious to push forward any means of bringing such an improved state of things into existence. As far as legislation goes, our action is one of examination and inquiry, and as far as executive administrative acts are concerned, we have already done our best to enforce the law."

There was a spirited debate in the Commons on Mr. Parnell's

Amendment to the Address; the Amendment being defeated by 304 to 181.   Mr. Parnell then brought in a Tenants Relief Bill, which had the support both of Mr. Gladstone and Mr. John Morley, but this was rejected on the 21st of September by 297 to 202 ; and then on the 25th idem Parliament was prorogued.

Nothing of moment occurred during the recess till on the 22nd of December, Lord Randolph Churchill resigned the Chancellorship of the Exchequer on a question of the Navy Estimates.

Lord Salisbury then very wisely made overtures to the Liberal Unionists, and as a result, Mr. Goschen, on the 3rd of January, 1887, agreed to join the Cabinet as Chancellor of the Exchequer. This gave undoubted strength to the Government, as well on account of Mr. Goschen's acknowledged genius as a financier, as on account of his position as a Liberal Unionist.

On the 12th of January Lord Iddesleigh, more familiar as Sir Stafford Northcote, died, and left a gap in the Conservative ranks.

On the 27th idem, Parliament met, and the debate in the Commons on the Address began the next day, and after seventeen nights the debate was closed by the application of the Closure.   The new Procedure Rules next occupied the attention of the House, and were passed after fourteen nights' debate.

On the 5th of March, Sir Michael Hicks-Beach, who held the Irish Secretaryship, was compelled to resign it on account of ill health, and Mr. A. J. Balfour was appointed in his stead.

The first thing the Government did with regard to Ireland was to introduce a Bill for the suppression of Crime.   This Bill was introduced in March, and passed the Commons on the 8th of July.

But while Lord Salisbury intended to have the law obeyed, he intended to remedy abuses wherever found ; accordingly, on the 31st of March, three days after the Crimes Act had been introduced in the Commons, the Irish Land Law Bill was introduced in the Lords. Speaking in one of the later debates, Lord Salisbury said of this Bill that the necessity for it arose from the insane policy of the Ministry of 1881 ; the great evils from which the farming class of Ireland suffered were want of capital and want of credit, and he feared that want of confidence and that instability were likely to increase.   The Government were trying to patch up a system which they had always condemned, and they regarded this Bill only as a partial solution.   After much debate, it finally passed both Houses on August 18th.

On the following day Lord Salisbury proclaimed the National League as a dangerous association under the Crimes Act. This roused Mr. Gladstone, who on the 25th idem moved for the withdrawal of the proclamation, but the motion was rejected the following night by 272 to 194.

On July 14, 1887, the Queen paid a marked compliment to Lord Salisbury, in honour of the Jubilee, by visiting him at Hatfield House, an engraving of which is given on page 87.

The following account of the visit, taken from the *Standard* of the following day, will be found interesting :—

"Among the 'stately homes of England' few, if any, possess a deeper historic interest, or awaken more pregnant antiquarian memories, than Hatfield House, the Hertfordshire seat of the Marquess of Salisbury. For nearly three centuries past the venerable pile has been one of the centres of English political and social life, and the associations which cluster round it are part of our national history. Kings have been entertained there with an hospitality little short of regal ; it was there that a princess, afterwards one of the greatest of English queens, was kept in semi-confinement ; and there also have been from time to time decided upon schemes of policy of vital importance to the Empire.   James I., Elizabeth, Oliver Cromwell, Charles I., George I., George IV., and Victoria, are amongst a few of the royal guests who have accepted the hospitality of the Lords of Hatfield since the early part of the seventh century, when the great founder of the House of Cecil, Lord Burleigh, had to surrender; with what grace he could, the noble demesne of Theobalds at Cheshunt, to which James I. had taken a fancy, in exchange for the Hertfordshire estate.   Ancient as is Hatfield House itself, some of its appurtenances can boast of a still higher antiquity, for what is now the principal stable was one the banqueting-hall of the Bishops of Ely, who held the estate, or the larger portion of it, down to the time of Henry VIII., and whose palace stood upon a part of the site occupied by the present structure.   The house is full of treasures of priceless value to the antiquarian and the student of art.   Visitors may see the gorgeously-carved and gilded bed in which James I. slept during one of his visits, the couch on which Oliver Cromwell is said to have rested, Queen

Elizabeth's saddle upon which she sat when reviewing her forces at Tilbury, just before the Armada hove in sight. Queen Elizabeth's cradle, too, is here, and her hat and silk stockings, and everywhere on the walls are pictures of surpassing interest, and, in many cases, of surpassing merit; while to students of history everything will be un-important in comparison with the wealth of manuscripts and books that fill the capacious cabinets ranged round the library. To the majority of visitors, however, the park is perhaps the chief attraction, and certainly no more beautiful sylvan scenery could be desired than that which is afforded by its umbrageous avenues of limes and oaks, venerable, some of them, with a growth of nearly ten centuries.

" Yesterday the long list of royal visits to Hatfield received a notable addition through the presence of the Queen, who attended a garden-party given by the Marquess and Marchioness of Salisbury in honour of the Royal Jubilee. Once before Her Majesty was at Hatfield, in 1846, when she was for a few hours the guest of the then head of the Cecil family. Yesterday, at the Queen's express desire, the affair was kept as quiet and as informal as is possible when Royalty is present.

" The Queen, who was accompanied by Prince and Princess Henry of Battenburg, the Grand Duke of Hesse, the Princesses Irene and Alix of Hesse, and the Hereditary Grand Duke of Hesse, left Windsor shortly after four o'clock, travelling *via* Acton and Canonbury over the Great Western and North London lines to Hatfield, which was reached at 4.45. Her Majesty was received at the station by the Marquess of Salisbury, Lord R. Cecil, Lord Colville of Culross (the Chairman), and Mr. Oakley (General Manager), of the Great Northern Company, and amidst enthusiastic cheering the Royal party entered two carriages, which, with fifteen horses—several of which were for the use of the equerries—had been sent over from Windsor in the morning. The guard of honour was furnished by the Herts mounted constabulary, under Colonel Daniells, and the same force, assisted by a detachment of men from the A Division of the Metropolitan Police, lined the approaches to the house. Her Majesty was again loudly cheered as she drove up the stately avenue, now lined with spectators, and repeatedly acknowledged the warmth of her reception. Dressed as usual in black, with a lilac aigrette in her bonnet, the Queen looked exceedingly well, and was evidently in the best of spirits.

" On arriving at the East Terrace Her Majesty was received by the

HATFIELD HOUSE—THE HOME OF THE CECILS.

Marchioness of Salisbury, and the members of the Royal family who had previously arrived, and conducted to the pavilion prepared for her, where, during the two hours of her stay, a number of the guests were presented to her.

" Only about a hundred and fifty invitations in all were issued, and these, apart from the Royal and official visitors, were accepted by the representatives of the principal county families, the number being thus limited in accordance with the Queen's express desire. The Princess of Wales and other Royal guests left by special train for London shortly after half-past six, but the Queen remained till nearly seven, driving down Fore Street to the station, amidst cheers which were renewed by the crowd in the station as the train left for Windsor, where Her Majesty arrived shortly after half-past eight."

The Government during the Session of 1887 managed to pass the Coal Mines Regulation Act and the Allotments Act, and on the 16th of September, 1887, Parliament was prorogued.

In October, the same year, the world knew that two of the most difficult questions in respect to our diplomatic arrangements with France had been satisfactorily settled. The Suez Canal is to be free to ships of war at all times, but no acts of hostility can be permitted within a certain distance of the Canal ; that is the one question. The other question concerns the New Hebrides. Australia was always protesting against France possessing this colony, and now by diplomatic arrangement France has promised to evacuate it. No praise is so sweet as the praise you have wrung perforce from an opponent. Therefore I think I cannot better end this sketch of Lord Salisbury's life than by quoting the tribute of *The Daily News* to Lord Salisbury's diplomacy : " Lord Salisbury is to be sincerely congratulated on the success of his diplomacy. . . . It seems to us that the course he has taken is a wise and statesmanlike one."